ASCENSION
DAY

ASCENSION DAY

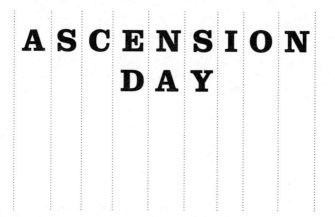

CHRIS DOLAN

review

First published in 1999
by REVIEW

An imprint of Headline Book Publishing

10 9 8 7 6 5 4 3 2 1

ISBN 0 7472 7545 9

Typeset in 13 on 15pt Perpetua by
Palimpsest Book Production Limited
Polmont, Stirlingshire

Designed by Peter Ward

Printed and bound in Great Britain by
Clays Ltd, St Ives, plc.

Headline Book Publishing
A division of Hodder Headline PLC
338 Euston Road
London NW1 3BH

For Maggi

Thanks to:
Moira
Emi, Gabriel, Paul, Kay, Louise
Mike Gonzalez, Mick Morton, Brendan Hughes,
Mike Alexander, Kathy Galloway, Geraldine Cooke,
Leslie Finlay, Charlie & Teresa
Without them this ascension'd never've got off the
ground

O N E

William's not a voyeur – but there's not much he can do
about the neighbours. He's out in his garden tending his
flowerbeds, mulling over how best to respond to this
morning's letter, and there they are, carrying on as though
they were in the middle of the Kalahari, surrounded by
unseeing bushland. They must be seventy if they're a day,
yet they saunter in and out of their uncurtained house
naked, lie shamelessly around their pool. This section of
Khomosdal has only recently been built and the hedges and
frangipanis are not tall enough to offer real seclusion. The
husband's nigh on twenty stone, the wife thin but with
loose flesh that sways when she moves. At the pool, he lets
his towel fall and she laughs, ooohs loudly at his flaccid and
small, compared to the rest of his bulk, penis, like it's the
first time she's seen it. They're always at it, kneading the
inside of each other's thighs, rubbing suntan oil down backs

and bellies. They happily shout Hello! over to William while sliding their hands under bikini straps and trunk bottoms, extracting them only to give an oily wave.

It's hard not to watch them, unless you do what William's wife has done – decree the back garden out of bounds, and sit out the front. There've been complaints, of course, but the elderly couple just shrug and say folk should mind their own business. William's not prepared to let his roses and bougainvillaea go to the dogs just because of embarrassing neighbours. And anyway, he admires them. Unusual for such a long-married man to be still peering openly, unashamedly at his partner. Whether she's fully dressed or naked, engaged in some mundane act or parading in front of him, his eyes seldom leave her. Once or twice William's caught the old man sitting, gazing longingly and uncomprehendingly at her while she sleeps on a chair or Lilo, as if sight itself could leach the essential meaning out of her.

He's always been a studier, William. Professionally, of numbers, but he has a layman's interest in all things scientific. Before emigrating almost forty years ago he examined the city he was born in, trying to find – somewhere in that nicotine-stained mess – the dear green place his father loved so much. In later life, he was honoured for his services to Industry and Politics. Raised his children to be serious-minded too: Libertina's now a rising star of the new government; Alphonse the youngest ever professor in the University of Southern Africa. No doubt his next-door neighbour'll be a political enemy, supporter of the old Pretoria days, but he's also a kind of fellow spirit, a scholar trying to discern in the raw material of his wife's body some secret, some formula. Today in particular, they make William think of Grace. Padding naked in the damp northern light, hair loose, trickling down her neck.

This morning's letter is the first news he's had of her in over twenty-five years. His only connection with the old country these days is the odd phone call from journalists who see a story on slow news days in the local-boy-made-good in far-off Namibia. He replies politely to their questions and from time to time his opinions are printed in the financial and business pages of the *Herald* or the *Scotsman*, sometimes even accompanied by an out-of-date photograph of himself looking, he thinks, suitably business-like.

Then, out of the blue comes this weird note from Grace's little blonde daughter. He has an image in his head of a child, tongue out in concentration, legs dangling from the kitchen table, scraping away at the notepaper. Morag, of course, must be at least forty now. It doesn't help, though, that the handwriting's chaotic and the contents of the letter bizarre. The work of some eternal daydreaming toddler.

After breakfast, he put the letter in his briefcase and went off to town to attend a meeting. Grace stayed with him all morning, stretching her naked arms and legs through agenda items on inward investment, pinning her hair up afterwards during chit-chat about fishing trips to the Skeleton Coast. She's still with him now, out here in his garden, standing by his side, about to get dressed again, while he waters and weeds.

Morag Simms' letter's brought back all sorts of memories. The streets. He can visualise perfectly the rain and those old streets. Villas squatting next to amputated blocks of tenements; red and blond sandstone scrambled up together. Things'll've changed, of course – how couldn't they after nearly half a century? But bet he could still find his way around. The trees won't have changed, will they? Huge things, standing soaking, too close to the buildings, branches shaking their fists against windows. He can still clearly remember the colours of these streets – dried-out terracotta window-frames and doors, faded magnolia-blond sandstone, ox-blood red.

This morning, on first reading the letter, he got a fright. Thought it was some cranky religious way of telling him that Grace had died. Well, she was older than him and God knows he's attending enough funerals these days, so it was a possibility. By the next page of the grubby letter, though, it was apparent that she was alive. Not in the best of health, but still kicking and being cared for by her daughter. God help her. William hadn't seen Grace in nearly forty years; never would again. He'd only known her for a few brief months, yet the relief he felt at her still being alive was as great as if he'd been given the all-clear himself from some awful illness.

He sits down on a deckchair in the shade of his garden shed; takes out the letter, rereads it and shakes his head. Poor Morag. You can almost hear the tears and the panic behind the barely legible words. The girl – woman – claims to have been the only witness of an extraordinary, inexplicable event. The tone of the letter is excitable, confused, probably even deranged, as she describes seeing her own mother rise up into the sky.

And not just her mother alone, mind, but three people. It's terrible, but William finds it hard not to laugh. A trinity of them, ascending up into the heavens above Glasgow from the top of Policy Road hill. Hardly the most hallowed of ground for such sacred goings-on. There was a raven-haired girl, a young bedraggled boy, kicking and snarling and swearing, and an older woman, who had the presence of mind to hold her skirt in modestly as she rose up off the ground. William got the impression that Morag knows who the other two were, but thankfully she doesn't go into detail. Just makes a meal of the fact that her mother was the older woman in the middle.

What on earth made her tell *him* of all people about this? Morag Simms can have no memory of him. He would-n't've thought Grace would've volunteered any info, and indeed Morag says in the letter that her mother doesn't know she's writing to him, and she doesn't want her to know either. Perhaps the poor woman thinks there was something miraculous in her apparition and she's writing to the whole world to bring them the good news. Perhaps it's a cry for help. Whatever, what a burden for poor Grace to carry so late in life! He decides he'll write back to Mrs Simms. It's only polite, and he'd like to help. Also, maybe he'll get some real news of Grace if the daughter replies. It feels like an omen, this unexpected, renewed contact. Should act upon it.

He puts the letter in its envelope, sits back in his deckchair and, staring up at the bright blue African sky, tries to imagine this boy and girl rising up off into the clouds with his Grace. Then he hears a snap of elastic followed by the silly, teenagerish laugh of his absurd neighbour. Perhaps, had things been different, William would have become like him, tirelessly pondering Grace's body; charting over the years its changes. Maybe he and Grace would've been the ancient lechers scandalising a neighbourhood somewhere. He remembers that Grace was supposed to have held her skirt around her knees as she rose up into the air, so maybe not. He couldn't for the life of him imagine what a Grace in her sixties would be like.

One thing he is certain of, though. No matter how much the woman next door parades around and lets her old man stare and touch and watch her, she'll still re-main a mystery to him. Just as Grace always was. Is. Even now, after all his success, William can't get that perfectly ordinary woman, and those Saturday mornings in Bunnahabhain Road all those years ago, out of his mind.

T W O

Right from his earliest memory his own city had always felt
foreign to him. His father is standing at the window of their
top-storey flat, pointing out over the rooftops and saying:
—What's that?

William would have been about four or so, just before
the war, and he followed the invisible line his dad's finger
zapped out across the sky.

—Houses? Clouds? Steeple? William guessed.

His father laughed and shook his head, then waggled his
finger and said, —No. My finger.

A favourite little joke of his father's. Then he itemised
for William a whole galaxy of wonderful things that could
be seen from that window. Factories, cranes, parks, the Art
Gallery and University towers. In this memory of William's
the factories pump and bellow like they do in cartoons,
expanding and contracting at the seams, groaning under

the weight of industry. Cranes raise their fists, the trees curtsy, the gallery stares haughtily back at him, and the turrets of the university take no notice, too engrossed with their own insides. William remembered following the clear line of his dad's work-mangled fingertip pointing to the Greatest Education System in the World, over here Fair-Minded People, and somewhere, glimmering through the trembling leaves of the oaks and elms of Kelvingrove Park, the March of Progress.

But William never saw this city of his father's. He had to conjure it up in his head, try to turn the rash of shrunken scrubs and black buildings like fossil stumps into his father's Greenest City in the World. When he was older, it occurred to him that his father had invented his wonderful city, lugged it on his back all the way from an impoverished island in the north and, exhausted, set it down here.

How can you feel part of a place that doesn't exist? William worked hard all his young life trying to get the answer to that. And he was getting somewhere, too: making friends, discovering places, developing theories. Even getting glimpses now and then – like the sun coming out and lighting everything up – of his father's city. Then Isobel accidentally pointed Grace out to him, and within a year he'd given up on his quest and begun his long exile.

He was twenty-three at the time, and his family had moved out of their old top-storey flat into Uncle Robert's large handsome semidetached in the city's west end.

Uncle Robert Grant had never married, saving every penny from the substantial salary he earned in Bangalore to bankroll his anticipated life as a returned sahib in Glasgow. When he died intestate his brother inherited both the house and his savings. William's father, however, saw nothing wrong with the family's poky flat in the sky, with its views out over the city, and refused to move into the big, spacious house. Nor would he touch his brother's savings, which he felt were ill-gotten. William and his mother and sister had to wait until he himself had passed on before they could enjoy the fruits of Robert's colonial labours. But by the time Isobel accidentally introduced William to Grace, he was the head of the family residing at number 29 Bunnahabhain Road, and about to complete his Master's Degree in Accountancy.

He'd always been good at maths – that ran in the family – and English. Given the need for financial expertise at home, accountancy seemed the most practical option. The English he'd learnt from his parents was an unruly affair, a peppery mix of Grant Gaelic, Doric on his mother's side, and Lowland Scots. Learning so many vernaculars from such a young age sensitised him to dialect and diction. By the age of fifteen he found he could identify not only the part of town a speaker came from, but which cluster of streets and, sometimes, if it was an area he knew well, even the individual street itself.

It became his party trick. Friends and acquaintances would test him, asking him where they came from, and by and large he would get it pretty well right. Even adding in, if the clues were strong enough, where their parents came from. He performed his trick in the university canteen where his classmates would bring in some stranger and William, like a palm reader, would work his magic on her or him. The specimen would talk for around five minutes, on any subject. William listened with furrowed brow, then he'd nod professorially, state his conclusions.

—You're fairly new to Glasgow. I'd say in second year. You were brought up in Ayrshire, but your parents – both of them? – are from the east coast. Not too far north. Angus?

He found, with practice, he could embellish this information, to everyone's delight.

—You live in a flat, but you didn't manage to get one near the university. South side, probably. I'd say your father had a fairly good job – your diction is quite clear – a teacher, perhaps?

He'd instantly recognise when someone was skewing their accent to suit either their own or others' views of them: most often middle-class boys crumpling their vowels and corrugating consonants to sound authentically working-class. Or country girls splitting their naturally pillowy pronunciation into sharp little shards of city brogue.

The total effect on his audience gave the impression that William was a man of profound psychological insight, second-sighted perhaps. But, despite the confidence with which he would hold court during these sessions, his feeling of not understanding a thing about the people around him grew rather than diminished. He could go anywhere, be with anyone, slip easily into their way of speaking. He could don dark glasses and a black polo neck and talk Ginsberg, Trocchi or Greco with arty types on the Byres Road. Or stroll into one of his father's old pubs in Maryhill Road, argue with the best of them about Puskas, Baxter and Joe Louis. But he never felt truly at home in any of these situations. Nor did he think that, beyond the niceties and formalities, could he strike any deep bond with these new, easily acquired friends. At twenty-three and in his final year of studying, he could wander freely around his home city, conversing in any of its many languages, without understanding a damn word anyone ever said.

It was Isobel who noticed Grace, and immediately wished she hadn't. Ever since their father had died, Isobel had made it her mission in life to see William settled and married. She sought out likely partners for him, and William tried most of them out, but the girls, despite his reasonable looks and intelligence, seemed frightened or put off in some way, and moved on. Isobel, however, wasn't discouraged. Her principal hunting ground at this time was the local kirk. Not for religious or moral reasons, but simply because there was a greater number of youngish, unmarried women at church than in any other social grouping.

It'd escaped her notice that Grace was wearing a wedding ring. But having made eye contact and stepped towards her, it was too late to back off. She abruptly let go of her brother's arm and approached her by herself. William shook his head, smiled to himself. This one was definitely not his type. Flat heels, calf-length floral dress with high collar, wool coat. Her hair, under a maidenly hat, was unkempt, folded back and showing signs of early greying. Once or twice, as she chatted to his sister, she looked over at William and smiled civilly.

She didn't appear at church the following week, thankfully. The next time he saw her was in Dumbarton Road. He was walking along in a dwam, working on an equation that had been forming in his mind.

In recent years he'd been trying out a mathematical line of enquiry to come to an understanding of the city around him. He called his starting point *The Agreed City*. That is, although each of its inhabitants perceived an entirely different city, there must be a base line upon which all of them agreed. This line he took as the physical city itself – the river with its clanking shipyards, dividing north and south; the centre and the east and west ends. The bridges, the architecture, the new towns being built all around the old city core, the presence of the people themselves.

She waved to him from across the road. He didn't

recognise her at first, but smiled politely anyway. Then she called to him and, hearing her voice through the traffic, he remembered who she was and also that she probably hailed from Greenock. She was standing in a shop doorway, like she'd come out for a quick smoke. Perhaps she worked in the shop, though she had no apron on. She smiled at him broadly when he crossed over the road and stood in front of her.

—Hello, he said.

—Hello?

A definite question mark. As if he was the one who had called to her and now she wanted to know why. He tried again.

—We met at church. At least we—

She laughed and put her finger to her lips, as if he had just let some secret out of the bag.

—I'm sorry, I don't know your name.

—Grace.

—Grace what?

—You tell me. I hear you're good at guessing games.

Where had she heard that? Surely not from Isobel. Some other churchgoer must have heard of his college-boy party tricks and mentioned it to her.

—Let me see. Henderson.

She laughed, as if the very idea was quite ridiculous.

—Ritchie? Ramsay?

She waited, still smiling at him, an infinite patience about her, like she'd be happy to stand there all day as he went through every possible surname until he happened upon the right one. There was no doubt she was from a very ordinary background, though her words carried the inflection of recent self-improvement. Her face was what Isobel called 'comely' and was clearly the face of a woman in her mid-twenties. But the dress, another version of the same floral-patterned, high-neck, low-hem she had worn the Sunday before, added ten years to her.

—Boyd. Shaw. Smith.

Then it dawned on him that he was looking in the wrong place. She was married. It wasn't like him to make such an elementary mistake. That shallow twang of hers, closing down some of her vowels – he needed another set of names, names from higher up the social order.

—Burnett. Lamont.

Both with the emphasis on the second syllable. Then she suddenly gave the game away, like she knew he was about to get it right and wanted to deny him his victory.

—Lapraik.

He'd never have guessed Lapraik in a thousand years. It didn't sound likely. Grace Lapraik. An odd, stunted rhythm to it.

—Can we count on your vote, then?

—Excuse me?

—Local elections, silly.

Then he noticed that the shop window behind her was bedecked with posters, rosettes and leaflets for the Labour Party.

—Are you running?

—Heavens no!

—Who then?

—My husband. George.

And she turned round and headed back into the shop. William was about to continue on his way when she popped her head back round the doorway.

—If you like, I'll give you the election sermon.

—OK.

—Next Wednesday then. Ten o'clock? The bakery tearoom along the road there?

She pointed eastwards along Dumbarton Road, stepped

back into the doorway, so that all that was left for him to say yes to was an unmanicured finger.

On a blurred, foggy Wednesday morning in March, he went along to the tearoom behind the bakery on Dumbarton Road to meet Mrs Lapraik over tea and scones. He listened patiently to her earnest politics, hearing his father's voice prising its way from a decade ago between her carefully measured words. He felt again the old desire to be convinced of the bright new future and his own place in it. Grace warned that the Conservative Government would be re-elected yet again so long as Gaitskell remained in charge of Labour's fortunes. Between odd little silences that embarrassed him but didn't seem to bother her, she explained all about her Constituency Party's plans. She herself was playing a lead rôle in the establishment of a childrens' home in Dudhope Road – in the teeth of local opposition. She worried that another national Labour defeat might set back plans for the home irredeemably, together with the rest of their proposed good work. Then she brought the conversation to an abrupt end, and they parted with William's whole-hearted agreement to vote for her husband at the local election, but declining to take part in the campaign itself.

    As they stood outside the bakery, turning collars up and adjusting hats against the rain, she said: —Same time next week? like they were old friends and had been meeting like this for years.

He expected, making his way to the bakery the following week – Bunnahabhain Road's trees responding to a spring there was no sign of yet in the steel sky and wet air – that the purpose of this meeting'd be to convince him to get actively involved in the people's party. In fact she spoke about herself and her family. Told how her husband was a plater on the lower Clyde until, spotted for his stalwart performance as shop steward, he was asked to stand as councillor. He served for two years in Gourock. (*Not* Greenock; William was disappointed at his deduction being short of the mark.) Now he was contesting one of Labour's key Scottish seats, Glasgow West.

And she talked about her little girl. Told him all about the child's antics. William told Grace a little about his own background. About the wee flat in the sky, the big house in the west, his sister and mother. Then talked about Macmillan and Bevan and Gaitskell and the Middle East, about Monroe and Connery and television, and, as the trams outside cranked by, about ridding the streets of their menace, and about the new towns that were providing proper homes in new estates for put-upon slum dwellers. There were still those little silences between them, when she would look idly around and then, suddenly, directly at him. A moment later she'd pick up from where she'd left off, enthuse about the plans for the modern-thinking home for children at risk in Dudhope Road, shake her head sternly at the thought of those west end residents who were up in arms against the idea. He, for the first time in his life, talked to another living soul about his ambition of finding a mathematical solution to a social question. He told her about *The Agreed City*, and she laughed, and so did he.

They talked freely about all manner of things in that tearoom at the back of the bakery. Sometimes having to raise their voices above the racket from the street outside and the shop customers shouting orders for cakes and breads and buns and rolls and the clatter of trays being slammed in and dragged out of the hot ovens. William sat back in his chair, fascinated as much by why she'd chosen him to talk to as by her conversation itself. He studied her, this woman who arrived each week in old-fashioned clothes, no makeup, hair haphazardly folded into a chignon with decorative but cheap pins: a bird of paradise, a Celtic cross. And every week he noticed that a flank of hair, seeded with early grey, escaped from the fold at the back of her head, curling down under the high collar of her dress, settling on the nape of her neck. As they sat together she regularly checked the buttons of her dress and talked in fits and starts, crossed and uncrossed her legs, not nervously but calmly, then from time to time would lean forward and talk *sotto voce* so that anyone nearby would think she was exchanging secret nothings with him, when in fact all she was saying was that her daughter had a cold or that her husband's campaign was going well.

Then, one Wednesday, she touched him, laid her hand for an instant on the back of his, while she was talking about some quite impersonal matter. He said nothing, but left his hand where it was in the hope that she'd return to it.

She never did, but when they stepped out into the sooty morning air, instead of confirming for the following week, she said: ——I've always wanted to see inside one of those big houses in Bunnahabhain.

——Then, please, pass by one day.

——Would Saturday morning be all right? Ten o'clock?

Grace would only have been about five or six years older than him, if that, yet he felt like a minor being sent on an errand. Having dictated the time and place she left him, like a pupil being set a task, to organise the details. They would meet, at his house, at the appointed time, which was when his mother and Isobel habitually went out shopping.

Had he told her that? He was sure he'd mentioned it, once at least, complaining about how seldom he got peace and quiet to study in.

He had no notion whatsoever what her feelings towards him really were. That one touch – the skin of her fingers fleetingly grazing his – was the only sign that the rendezvous in his house might mean more than a simple change of venue for their weekly chats.

But he couldn't be sure. So he tidied his bedroom, just in case. He also bought scones and biscuits – hid them in his wardrobe like articles to be ashamed of – in case pleasant conversation over tea was all she had in mind. He debated with himself whether or not to tell Isobel and his mother that he would be receiving a visit from Grace Lapraik. Perhaps she would expect them to be there after all.

On the morning of the visit, he transferred the teabreads from his room on to a cake stand in the living room, arranged two chairs at either side of the table, set out cups and saucers and plates. The table sat in the bay window and he half closed the curtains so he and Grace could sit there without being seen, but with enough light from outside so as not to give the impression of concealment. Then he went back upstairs to his room, switched on his bedside lamp and closed the curtains completely.

She arrived about ten minutes late, dressed in her Sunday clothes. A slightly better coat than usual, a less battered hat, the dress she'd worn the day he first saw her at church – its high, puritanical neck final proof that her visit was purely social. She looked at him for a moment before smiling, almost surprised, as though he were the last person she'd expected to find there. Perhaps she'd expected Isobel or his mother to answer the door.

—Hello, she said, and stepped inside, as if she were passing a distant acquaintance on the street. In the hallway she had a good look round, while he waited for her at the living-room door, annoyed at her interest in his family.

At the table, Grace sat down and shrugged her coat off on to the back of the chair. The flank of grey-peppered hair had already worked its way out of her tight chignon and spilled down the back of her neck into her dress. She looked up at him expectantly. He offered her the cake stand.

—Please, have a scone.

—No thanks.

—Biscuit?

She waved her hand.

—Give me a minute and I'll bring in the tea.

—Not for me. Thanks.

He felt wrong-footed. The clean tablecloth, crockery, scones and conserves embarrassed him. She didn't even let him off the hook by inviting him to go ahead and have some tea himself, but continued to sit, smiling at him, waiting – he had no idea for what. He sat down opposite her, on the edge of his seat, and began with their usual pleasantries: how were things with her, with her girl, how was the election campaign going? To each question she replied with a wave of her hand or a simple 'fine'. When he ran out of questions, she directed her gaze momentarily away from him, looked out the window.

Then she smiled broadly and asked: —And how are your calculations going?

—Actually, I'm quite pleased with my progress, he said, although he wasn't. He hadn't made any progress whatsoever recently, had even for the first time lost faith in the entire project. By the look on her face he could see she thought the subject amusing, and he tried to be bright and relaxed about it.

—I really think I've got beyond the initial premise of *The Agreed City* to the next stage.

Grace nodded sagely. He knew he couldn't do his arguments justice in this situation, but that wasn't the point. The point was to break the ice; perhaps fill the whole morning up until Isobel and his mother returned.

—I've represented the agreed elements of the city by the variable n, so that n equals the prima-facie facts of the city – north, south, social class, character, et cetera.

And she nodded again, a little too vigorously. Those not involved in methodical, logical inquiry were so dismissive of the simplicity of things. It was as if science were self-evident, that things could be taken for granted, without being quantified and tested to make sense of them. All his life he had been stunned by the confidence of those around him. Everyone so convinced of their view of the world without ever submitting it to rigorous examination. If she wasn't taking his investigations seriously, then neither would he.

—The vast majority of the population as far as I can see, are quite happy living in the city of what I call the *Lowest Common Denominator*. Which leads me to a complex equation. Put simply, it could be represented by $x = \frac{y}{n}$ where x = the ultimate nature of the city, y = the physical, simple reality of it – and n = the composite of what everyone else believes, or knows, about the city. In order to discover x, of course, we must first define y . . .

But Grace put her finger to her lips and silenced him. She got up and came round the table towards him. She crouched down beside his chair and the smile faded from her face. She touched his cheek, then gently took his hand. Her palm was rougher than he expected, like the regular grain of varnished pine. She put her other hand behind his elbow, directing him slowly out of his chair. She leant towards him and the loose strands of her hair brushed his neck.

And she whispered: —Tell me afterwards.

The pattern of Wednesday mornings in the tearoom gave way to Saturdays at home. Grace arrived, always in her Sunday best; William provided the tea and cakes which they seldom ate. On the first few occasions Grace broke the ice, getting up and going to him. Then, for a couple of weeks, William took the initiative. Finally, it was done by a certain look they perfected between themselves, and they met halfway, kissed and walked to the door.

Upstairs in his curtained room, dustily lit by an old Indian bedside lamp inherited from Uncle Robert, its bright saffron shade wearied by the years into nutmeg, they'd kiss again and Grace would sit on the bed, tilt her head for William to run his fingers through her hair, down into her loosened collar to the nape of her neck. In the early days, they undressed sitting at either side of the bed, back to back, stealing glances. For a while they experimented with undressing each other, but soon settled on undressing themselves again but standing close, face to face.

Throughout their few months together, undressing was their most important ritual. Grace shedding those floral-patterned dresses, the fumble of detaching the pins from her hair, sitting to release buttons and peeling away nylons. She remained Mrs Lapraik, the churchgoing politician's wife down to her – hardly provocative but plain and overwashed – underwear. Only at the moment when she pushed her head back to look solidly at him, her arms behind her back to loosen her bra, did she become Grace.

Then raising herself up, thigh muscles swelling briefly, to slip off underpants, she'd look down at her naked self, as if she was surprised to find that she had the most beautiful body in the world.

She hadn't. William, during those silent stripping sessions had time to drink her in, commit her to memory. Those three brief hours – two, discounting the time they took reaching his room and getting back downstairs to wait for Isobel and his mother – seemed to him like eternities. Having freed herself from her Lapraik clothes Grace would sit there on the edge of the bed, looking down at herself. Not in shame or false modesty, but like she was silently coaxing her body, as you would a small animal or child. She would find reasons before or after lovemaking to move around the room, and William felt that she was not only doing it for him, but out of the sheer pleasure of stepping, bending, reaching, combing in her own nakedness, like she were trying on a comfortable and stylish new outfit she could only dream of having the money to buy.

In stature, she was shortish, as if generations of west-coast toil had weighed heavily and compressed some slenderer prototype. Her back was strong and straight and her shoulders symmetrical crescents, her thighs tough and competent, arms long, vigorous. Her body fat was concentrated around the hips and buttocks, but not dense enough to conceal the stirring and twisting of muscles beneath compliant skin.

He watched the clench of her leg and arm muscles as she moved freely around him, the way her face changed, slowly, slowly, from entering the room, relaxing as she undressed, becoming almost sleepy as she lay beside him, her body indolent. Though they never spent an entire night together, the murky light in his curtained room at ten in the morning felt like dusk, and after making love they would slumber, lying for a few minutes, curled around each other, and whenever William felt the need to speak, she muzzled him with drowsy kisses.

It was Grace's idea that, instead of her scurrying away after sex, she should wait, dignified, for William's mother and sister to return. And so, each week they would go downstairs and talk like acquaintances until the shoppers came home.

His mother, so far as he knew, never suspected anything, but Isobel was not so easily fooled, and William braced himself for her disapproval. In fact she became their accomplice. She sat each week at the head of the table surrounded by her mother, brother and her brother's mistress, dispensing tea and nuggets of local gossip. Within a month, William no longer had to set the table or buy in the teabreads: all that was done for him. Isobel tidied up his room, freshened the air by leaving his window open for an hour or two, closed it again and pulled the curtains fully flush. Then she took her mother out, extending the lovers' time together by not returning until well after one. Nothing was said between them, but Grace couldn't have failed to notice these little services. Although she was the party with so much more to lose, she was less discreet than William was. Sometimes even sharing a conspiratorial smile with Isobel.

Marriage for William was still Isobel's main task, but by now she'd discovered she had a new talent. Young men and women had begun to consult her, outside church or in the street, seeking her advice, or even active involvement, in their search for a partner. She'd give hints on how to dress and where to go of an evening or for a pleasant afternoon's walk; subtly matching lonely hearts up with one another.

She was still determined to find a proper wife for her brother, but clearly saw no harm in his affair with Grace in the short-term. She continued to point out eligible girls and introduce him to the ones that interested him. She took less and less interest in her own romantic life, and more in matchmaking for others. With William taking charge of all things financial and legal in the household, Isobel utilised her own organisational skills on the arithmetics of the heart. By the time her brother abruptly left the country, she could claim one wedding, one engagement, six or seven long-standing amours, not to mention brief flirtations and dalliances.

For a few months Grace, William and Isobel and their mother lived peaceably from Saturday morning to Saturday morning, with only one interruption. William attended his classes, though was less inclined to study at home at night. Mrs Grant concerned herself with her failing health. Grace attended church semiregularly, and was seen around the area with her chubby little ringletted daughter. She continued to canvass on her husband's behalf. No one minded her enthusiasm for extending the city's plans to build bright, new estates in the north and east. But when the Corporation bought the house in Dudhope Road that she had chosen, to make a reality of her dreams for a progressive-thinking children's home, she began to encounter real local hostility.

The interruption in their Saturday mornings came with George Lapraik's successful election as Councillor for Glasgow West. It was only a minor inconvenience. Two Saturday mornings were missed – one immediately after the victory and another two weeks later when the Lapraik family took themselves off for a well-deserved break in Millport. During all the months that William had been seeing Grace, first in the tearoom, then at home, he had never questioned how she had managed to skip away or what she did with her little girl. After she returned from her weekend at the seaside he did ask her, but she waved the question away and confirmed for the following Saturday.

It was a decent spring in the year of 1959, sun and rain in equal measure, turning Bunnahabhain Road into a rainforest, bushes swelling into thickets, trees bloating, obscuring the little extra light the sky had to offer. William went out during those weeks with a nineteen-year-old girl Isobel had chosen for him from an art night-class she attended. With Saturday mornings to look forward to he felt almost happy. The city seemed less frightening to him. The streets smelt different: coffee and fresh cigarette smoke instead of coal and damp clothes and ash. Once or twice he and his girlfriend passed Grace and little Morag in the street, and Grace would smile warmly at them, nodding her approval.

But his mother's health was deteriorating, and his final exams loomed. Isobel was getting impatient, making it obvious she thought Grace and her brother's little interlude was lasting too long. Grace, busier with Morag, and her position on the board of the children's home, from time to time had to cut short their weekly sessions. She seemed distracted on occasion, taking less delight in walking slowly around his half-lit room, revelling in her nakedness. Things were not going well for William and, then, to top it all, the Grants suddenly had to pay for the privilege of residing at Bunnahabhain Road.

Uncle Robert's career and tragic early death – when William and Isobel were only children – were the stuff of myth in the Grant family. How, within a few years of arriving in India to work as an engineer and manager on the railways, he had been appointed stationmaster for Bangalore. How his luck ran out just before the British administration did. In 1946, attempting to keep a protest march of Gandhi's noncooperation movement out of the city, he ordered all trains to be halted a mile short of the city's boundaries. Resolute, but in the spirit of arbitration, he set out along with other British top brass to confront the rebel leaders. The demonstrators had taken an oath of nonviolence, and it was not they who caused his death but, without trains to take them into the city, they marched the shortest route through farmlands, accidentally frightening a herd of cattle into stampede that met Uncle Robert head-on.

He was only thirty-five at the time and unmarried. One or two photographs had been returned with his belongings from India and he looked quite the dashing hero. Clark Gable moustache, slicked-back hair, suits more Edwardian than forties. Legends were made from the scraps of rumours and reports that reached Glasgow of his Indian exploits, in business, sport and love. Isobel particularly had a fascination for him. She kept his photographs in her room together with the few tattered documents that were all that was left of his short life. In company she liked to tell tales, based on rumours she'd heard from her mother, of Uncle Robert's many lady friends – English duchesses, American starlets, native serving girls.

But if Janki Devi Srikanthan was to be believed, Isobel's idea of Uncle Robert was very far from the mark. Mrs Srikanthan was one of – according to her, the *only* – woman in his supposed harem of serving girls. She denounced him as a weak-minded bully. The family solicitor showed William all the documents, pages of sordid details that suddenly came flooding in from the Indian subcontinent, threatening the Grant family's peace and calm.

He read the accusations of rape – Uncle Robert having first violated her, Srikanthan claimed, when she was fourteen years of age. He continued to abuse the girl for the next five years. She was the only woman he could make love to because, in her opinion, she was the only woman over whom he felt total control. The documents stated that Mrs Srikanthan had been effectively 'sold' by her father to Robert Grant; that she had no family or friends in Bangalore, and was therefore completely at her employer's mercy.

Two years before his death, however, after what she maintained was a brutal bout of violent abuse, Robert Grant broke down in tears and pleaded for her forgiveness. As proof of his sincerity he scribbled on a sheet of paper that she was to all intents and purposes his wife, and from then on he would treat her as such. Within a few weeks he had succumbed to his old ways, and Janki finally made her escape. Seven years later, living in Jaipur, she married and settled down. It took another six years before she and her husband showed a lawyer the thumbed, stained and ragged oath. And yet another couple of years of research and graphology comparisons passed before the tropical storm rattled the shutters of 29 Bunnahabhain Road.

William tried to keep the details of the Srikanthan claim for their property and inheritance from Isobel and his mother. Grace listened patiently to his worries and drove a middle line, pointing out the justness of the Indian woman's claim, but sympathising with William's predicament. William's lawyer advised him that the Srikanthan claim was not to be taken lightly. Her legal representatives were, he said, pretty nifty. The best advice he could give was to offer the woman a settlement out of court.

About this time, Grace had begun bringing a little makeup bag with her on Saturday mornings. It began as a joke. Laughing and chasing him one morning, she dabbed a little powder on his face, then on her own. Before long she was painting elaborate masks on the two of them. At the mirror she would stencil in black kohl, long Egyptian eyebrows that curled from the bridge of her nose to her temples. She etched out her own lips in dark browns or blacks, his in deep reds and ochres. She made their eyelids brooding, cheekbones severe, their foreheads delicately patterned. She cajoled him into trying his hand at it too, and soon, after they had undressed, they began talking and laughing and painting each other's face and body. It seemed to free them up, these masks – the old Mrs Lapraik and William Grant obliterated, and in their place new people, strangers at every meeting. They lay there together, not quite naked any more, feeling emboldened by the creations they had made of one another. Sometimes they only had time to wipe away the makeup from their faces before Isobel brought Mrs Grant home. Downstairs with the ladies, they enjoyed the secret of their illustrated bodies – backs, breasts and buttocks embellished in a prism of colours.

Isobel's impatience finally reached a head. One Sunday morning in May she was visibly perturbed, in more of a rush than usual, irritated by their mother's slowness and dependency.

—In the name of God! she barked at the old woman, who looked up at her sorrowfully. She had been out of temper lately with William too. Muttering loudly in his hearing while opening his windows and bundling his cosmetic-rainbowed sheets into the washing machine. For a week or so she'd been enquiring pointedly about the night-class girlfriend she'd found him.

They went to church as usual. At the end of the service, Grace not turning up, she sought out another young woman and insisted they all walk home together. She led them the long way round, despite the snell wind, down towards Dumbarton Road then back up the hill, through Dudhope Road. But they still arrived home too early. Coming round the bend towards number 29, William saw two people exit the driveway of the Grants' house and clear off down the road in the opposite direction. He was about to shout and give chase when he realised he recognised them. One was an old boyfriend of Isobel's, the other a woman Isobel had once tried to pair William off with. He said nothing to Isobel, but marched angrily ahead, into the house. He went straight up to his room, but found it untouched.

He then checked Isobel's room and stood at the top of the stairs waiting for her to come up, his rage mounting. She took her time downstairs, settling her mother, putting on the kettle, but finally came up to face him. He stood staring into her room. The sheets on her bed were not ruffled by love and longing the way his were on a Saturday, but in a mess; the smell left hanging in the air sour, not peppery like the afterglow of Grace.

—How dare you?

—You're the last person to complain, she hissed. He'd meant to tell her off, but saw at once that her anger was much greater than his. He was shocked, found himself on the defensive.

—There's no comparison between the two things.

He kept his voice even and quiet, almost scared of her.

—And what precisely might the difference be?

—Don't be ridiculous, Isobel. It's perfectly obvious.

—That it's all right for you to sleep with a married woman in your own house behind your mother's back, but not for two single people to sleep together in the home of a perfect stranger?

—Hardly strangers! I know them both.

—So you'd've been happier had they been total outsiders? I'll bear that in mind.

It was the first argument of any significance they'd ever had, and William was surprised how bereft he felt once she had stormed into her room, slammed the door in his face. In all his years of searching for other people to study at close quarters he had never considered for a moment speculating about his own sister. The two of them grew up together – he ought to have had a clearer insight into her than any other person in the world. Why had she supported him so solidly all these years, wasted so much energy planning his life out for him?

Even now Isobel didn't stop doing her little favours for Grace and William, but she carried them out with a detached sense of duty, weekly chores that, much as though she'd rather not do them, she knew that if she didn't they'd never get done. Grace said nothing about the new atmosphere in the house. Never commented on Isobel's sudden absence from the table in the living room when they came down from their lovemaking, or wondered out loud why she never smiled at her in church or in the street any more.

William's mother's health took a sudden turn for the worse and the doctor ordered her into hospital for tests. It was taken for granted that any treatment would be done privately rather than having her wait in a National Health queue. But money was beginning to become a real worry and, with his final accountancy exams pressing, William felt snowed under, agitated and depressed.

On Saturday mornings, when his vexation vented itself sexually, Grace colluded, retaliating and grappling with him, until at times he felt as if each of them were fighting their own private battles; using the other as a decoy, a surrogate. Finally, rolling sweating away from each other, William would feel the need to apologise; Grace did not.

—Sorry, he said to her once.

And then she laughed and said:

—Why? We make angels and devils sing in harmony. And they both laughed together.

Still, her behaviour continued to change. Before, she had moved around the room for both his sake and her own, finding reasons to stretch out for things so that her shoulder muscles rippled and wedged. Now, it seemed she performed the ritual purely for herself. Later, downstairs, she was always supportive of him in his troubles – his sister's behaviour, his mother's illness, their finances, his exams – but he sensed her maintaining her position, stepping back from the problematic world of the Grants.

He spent most of his weekdays running between the university library, the family lawyer and doctor, and the bank. He didn't tell Isobel that their dwindling inheritance couldn't withstand paying out for their mother's medical costs *and* paying off Mrs Srikanthan. No money had come into the family since their father's death – their funds would be decimated by two such large disbursements in the same year. Isobel would only have criticised his handling of their affairs. And anyway, this was precisely the sort of thing a decent accountant was supposed to be on top of. If he were to succeed in the world outside he would need to be able to resolve this kind of situation as a matter of course.

He didn't have much time, or inclination, for his private calculations until, passing the shop front where he had first talked to Grace, he remembered their initial conversation. Just as, trying to guess her name, he had been looking in the wrong place, he realised that he'd been looking in the wrong place too for the solution to the problem of the city. Instead of searching for something that was there but which he couldn't detect, he should be looking for something conspicuous by its *absence*. Despite his problems at home, he found renewed energy now, late at night or during boring lectures, for the quest for his father's city, in the middle of all this muddle and difficulty.

The last Saturday in May, Grace arrived as usual. They sat at the table, buttered the scones and sliced the bread for the afternoon tea they'd later share with Isobel and Mrs Grant. These moments had become important to them, the only time they spent alone together outside his bedroom. They worked in a spirit of intimacy – glances and touches, their bodies wisping one another. It was their time to play married couple, engage in mundane, domestic activity. On this particular morning, the table set and ready for tea, they took each other's hand as usual at around twenty past ten, made their way upstairs.

They undressed slowly and in silence, watching each other strip away their lives and the city and the people around them. Both naked, Grace sitting on the bed, William kneeling between her thighs, they were holding each other's gaze and touching again, their gentleness simmering into lust, when they heard the main door downstairs open. They both knew it was Isobel – her anger was bound to erupt sooner or later – and that she was on her way up to make a scene. Yet they couldn't move. They heard her footstep on the stair, but they didn't jump apart. They stayed where they were, motionless, not knowing what to do. Only when Isobel opened the door without knocking did Grace move away from him, clasping her legs tightly together and bringing her arms round to hide her breasts. In those two simple movements, she draped drab Mrs Lapraik over herself. With his elder sister in front of him, condemning him, William became slowly aware of, horrified by, his own nakedness and still semierect penis. As she spoke, Isobel alternated her look regularly between Grace and William, her face stiffening with repugnance when her eyes met his.

—Have I not been good to you, William?

He said nothing, and she turned to Grace.

—Haven't I been your friend ever since you came to Glasgow, Grace Lapraik?

William could feel the tiniest nod of assent from Grace.

—Not that I minded. I was quite happy making my brother and my friend happy. But you've abused my good nature. When the whole thing comes to light, you two'll walk scot-free and it'll be me who'll carry the can.

William looked at Grace, to see her reaction to his sister's words. Curled on the end of the bed, trying to crush her nudity away, she was the picture of shame and guilt. He wanted her to do something. Stand up and nakedly defend herself and him against Isobel's martyrdom; or perhaps dress herself nonchalantly, deal with Isobel woman to woman, dismiss her.

—It always comes back to the big sister, doesn't it? Trying to keep the family together. I have to carry you all, and what thanks do I get? You've done nothing in return, William. And as for you—

Grace curled in a little tighter.

—I expected more.

For the first time she let her gaze linger on Grace. A disappointed, sad expression, not the despising stare she'd been directing at William. Grace looked up and, for a moment, relaxed under that gaze. William felt the two women were communicating in a way that excluded him, made his nakedness, his presence, unimportant.

Isobel stayed in the doorway. She held her arms close in against her sides, only her fingers moving, clenching, no part of her body extended across the invisible line she'd drawn for herself. She tossed her bob of brackish hair away from her eyes and cheeks, with a brittle flick of the neck. Most of the time she spoke to the empty area between Grace and William, dropping her angry words into the space between them, forcing them apart.

—Isn't it about time you spoke to your husband?

She glanced down at Grace.

—Before someone else does.

Then she backed off, took hold of the door handle.

And finally, addressing the entire room, the fixtures, Uncle Robert's lamp, the world beyond the curtained windows, she asked, —What payment do *I* get in all of this?

She'd kept her voice low and steady throughout the visit, and now that she was gone it was as if she had never been there. Just those whispered, damning words hanging in the air around William and Grace.

With Isobel gone, the main door downstairs banging behind her, Grace didn't pull her clothes on hastily, as William had expected. He sat a little away from her, tried to laugh. But they were embarrassed, naked like that, their legs clenched tight. The whole room rebuked them: Grace's makeup case lying in wait on the bedside table, a slur; the prim, undisturbed sheets scandalised; the dim, curtained light soiling the air. Then they dressed, not facing away from each other – that would have been too contrite, too much of an admission – but it was a joyless affair. Closing the door behind them they shut it on the naked, painted lovers, strangers to them now.

For form's sake, Grace waited for tea and biscuits with the Grant ladies as usual. Mrs Grant gave no indication of having noticed a change in the atmosphere, except to watch, curious, as Isobel swanned graciously around the table, making a fuss over Grace as if she were an un- expected, and not wholly welcome, guest. The ordeal over,

William walked Grace to the door and down the drive.

At the gate he asked her, hopelessly,

—Next Saturday?

And to his surprise she answered,

—Yes.

That night, and every other night after that until he finally left the country, William couldn't bear to go up to his room until he was certain of being so tired that he would fall asleep immediately. Isobel'd taken their mother into hospital for her tests the Monday after the débâcle with Grace, and the old lady's absence made the house unbearable. He avoided Isobel as much as possible, spending his time in the university library trying to catch up with his studies. On the Wednesday, coming home late, and passing Isobel's room, he caught the rancid, unsettling smell of other people's sex. On the Thursday he had to settle the Srikanthan claim, paying out £700, which he reckoned must be a fortune in Jaipur but which his solicitor advised him was a lot less than the legal costs of a case he was in no way certain to win.

The family was all but bankrupt. All three of them were costing money and earning none. William's tutors at the university had warned him that, on the basis of the quality of his work over these last few months, far from the first he and they were hoping for, he was facing the indignity of a third-class degree. That'd never get him a job well paid enough to sort out the family's finances. On the Friday, instead of studying, he walked the streets around Uncle Robert's semi, trying to decide what to do. Climbing Policy Road hill and peering at the grimy tenements on Dumbarton Road, inspecting the work being done on Grace's children's home on Dudhope, he was aware all the time of absence. As if he had already left the city and it was his own absence he was feeling.

He got back to Bunnahabhain tired and distracted. He would make no decisions about his future until the next morning, when he'd speak to Grace. Until he was calm and secure and wrapped up in her arms in his curtained room. But, when the morning eventually came, after a long and sleepless night, and after Isobel had gone out at ten o'clock to visit their mother in hospital, it wasn't Grace who stood at the door when he opened it, but George Lapraik.

—Good day, Lapraik said, handing him his hat, as though he were the doorman at the City Chambers.

William had seen Lapraik a few times before, with Grace and their little girl, out and about in the streets. It had never occurred to him to look closely at the man. He was surprised now at the Councillor's height, his leanness. He'd never noticed the neatly cut beard before, nor the sombre suit, the pale green sad eyes. What really surprised him, though, wasn't the detail of the man, but the sheer reality of him. Lapraik stooped as he entered and uttered some words that William didn't catch, but heard in them a serious, man-to-man tone that indicated some business to settle between the two of them.

Throughout her time with William, Grace had mentioned her husband often, and never with any trace of rancour or remorse. William had never felt jealous of him. Even though, recently, he had begun to wish for something more between Grace and himself, he had never considered George as standing in their way. It had never crossed his mind that *he* might have been standing in George's way. What William and Grace shared had nothing to do with anyone else. It lay outwith the normal everyday drift of the city, affected nobody but them.

George, holding his head too high, chin tightly locked, made his way past William into the house and, just as Grace had done on first entering, inspected the hallway closely. Then he turned to William.

—I don't want to fight.

The notion was absurd, and left William wordless.

—I've been informed of your friendship with my wife.

He spoke as if he were addressing a corporation meeting, admitting some shoddy piece of party mishandling which had to be brought out into the open. William found himself putting on a concerned face, not knowing how to act in the situation. He considered challenging Lapraik on his information, but rejected the idea. Either Grace herself had told him – though why she should have, he had no idea – or Isobel had. He thought of debating with him the precise nature of the friendship, but Lapraik would never be able to appreciate William's point of view. In the end, he merely nodded gravely, dumbly, and waited for Lapraik to speak.

—Grace wishes to remain with me.

Lapraik's series of simple assertions left William with nothing to do but nod and react, shake his head. Grace's name sounded out of place in that stern, angular mouth; wrongly pronounced, the vowel too short, consonants too hard. The word snapped on his lips, breaking it. It was clear now, though, that husband and wife had discussed William and his relationship with Grace, and were on the same side.

Lapraik stood looking at him, waiting for a response. The man was, after all, a democrat. It said so on all the pamphlets delivered round the doors, celebrating the politician's capacity for listening, for taking on board the opinions and points of view of the people.

—Of course she does. I never expected her not to.

It was true – he had never had any expectation of Grace leaving her family for him. Had made no plans for a future for himself and Grace. But he was worried by the easiness in his own voice. He didn't want to offend this serious man by seeming to shrug off his wife.

—I'm sorry.

The words sounded ridiculous, but Lapraik seemed to accept the apology, raising his eyebrow and nodding as though they had come halfway to a deal. William wanted to take him by the arm, lead him to a chair and explain that, really, they were talking about two different Graces. Even their names were pronounced differently. The Grace that came to his room on a Saturday morning had nothing whatsoever to do with Mrs Lapraik. Her actions did not in any way compromise the wife of the good Councillor. And that he himself, William, had not taken anything that belonged to him. The situation was merely a matter of appearances: public relations rather than substantive policy.

—What we have to decide, you and I, is where we go from here.

—Excuse me?

He had hoped that Lapraik's statements of the facts and his own apology had brought the embarrassing matter to an end. He expected George would feel honour bound to make a threat or two, be the responsible father and politician, give William a dressing-down, leave it at that. It even occurred to William that it might be possible to salvage something of the affair with Grace, rethink their schedule, find another place and time to meet, shed their outer selves again, without offending this man whom neither of them had anything against. But Lapraik continued to speak as though he were addressing a political opponent.

—I have an offer to make. It's my understanding that your family is under some financial pressure at present. I'm in a position to come to your assistance.

This new, condescending, heavier-accented tone

reminded William of his father. He shook his head and put up his hand.

—No need for that.

—Oh, but there is. I want an agreement with you. I want both parties – you and me – to sign up to it. Signed, sealed and delivered.

—You can have any agreement you wish. No payment is necessary.

Lapraik laughed. A practised laugh. One that he used frequently, no doubt, in negotiations to move the agenda on.

—Five hundred pounds.

Where would George Lapraik get such a sum of money from? His wife dressed as though they were as poor as church mice. His own suit was worn and frayed. Surely the man couldn't keep a certain amount of savings aside for just such a contingency.

—I really have no idea why you'd want to offer me money.

George stepped a little closer to him, leant his head down.

—So that you'll fuck off out of me and my wife's way.

THREE

On William's first day in Africa he sat in a café watching, in the middle of a busy junction of Moroccan streets, a stately policeman, epaulettes shimmering, earnestly directing the traffic. He waved cars forward, held his palm up imposingly to halt others, kindly signalled to fearful pedestrians. And all the while buses and lorries careered recklessly around him, people jaywalked and jumped out in the fleeting spaces between vehicles, horns blared, angry faces poked out of wound-down windows to exchange insults. But no one crashed. The crossroads had an order of its own. No one paid a blind bit of attention to the officer, waving and signalling with impressive dignity. For the rest of his life not a day would go by without William rejoicing in the flesh and blood, and the possibilities, of Africa.

His professor at the university had been helpful. Family and financial problems of hard-working students couldn't be helped. The professor reckoned the best accountants start at the bottom, work their way up. A degree was not imperative. It'd do William good, getting his hands dirty at the administrative coalface. He gave him a letter of reference to the company he himself had worked for years ago in German South-West Africa, secured him passage on a returning uranium ship to Johannesburg, with a twelve-hour stopover in Casablanca. Within a month of leaving Glasgow William had made his way from Lüderitz to Windhoek and had started work in the accounts department in his professor's old uranium-exporting company.

William immediately took to Windhoek – not a single entity but a conglomeration of different, possible cities: the impeccable streets and glistening new buildings of German Windhoek; grudging, fearful Afrikaans Windhoek; Lutheran Windhoek, earnestly hoping to lash together the precarious sides of this lean-to city. The Windhoek that the Ovambo and the San people saw rise up out of the bush of its own accord, pre-peopled with a translucent population. And finally, South African Windhoek, scorching in Pretoria's distant white sun.

No one would have foreseen that William's real life's work would be in politics. Perhaps he was paying homage to Grace, or trying to make amends for what he'd done to her husband. Or maybe he just detected that change was in the air. Lena – the German-born woman who'd become his wife – was every bit as political as Grace. She took him to see the Old Location, once the site of Windhoek's African heart, until the soldiers came, declared the houses slums, moved the people out. Lena showed him all that was left of a thriving community – a single crucifix for all those who died there, trying to resist. William thought of Grace and her ideals for bright new estates outside a city, thousands of miles to the north.

His new-found politics lost him a few friends and customers, but it brought others in their place, and he was surprised to find himself playing an active part in the coming-together of things.

In forty years there were only two letters from Isobel. The first, about a year after he left, to inform him of their mother's death. The second, nine years later when William was already a respected reformer. His son, Alphonse, was at school and his daughter, Libertina, in the care of a part-time nanny. The family were doing well, living in Pioneer Park, provoking black terror in the hearts of their neighbours by entertaining leading members of the South-West Africa People's Organisation – sometimes even the likes of John da Otto and Toivo ja Toivo.

Isobel needed help. Her business – what she termed a 'dating agency' – was in trouble. She assured William that it was all very tasteful, Uncle Robert's semi housing Parisian-style tea dances for lonely west end gentlemen and ladies. Unfortunately she had gone into business with a partner, who had let her down badly. He'd agreed to pay for redecorating the room where they entertained their clients, then reneged on his promise. He'd also organised, in her absence, an evening of entertainment that had got out of hand. The letter didn't give details, but the police had been called out. Isobel was confident it would all sort itself out, but if William'd be kind enough to advance her £1,000 and send it, along with a letter stating her good character, that'd be a great help. He doubted a reference from such a close relative would be of much use, but sent off the money and the requested letter by return anyway. She finished off the letter by bringing him up to date on the Lapraik family.

George Lapraik died not so long ago after a protracted and, I believe, distressing illness. The daughter is a fine big healthy girl, if a little withdrawn. I hope I can now renew my old friendship with Mrs Lapraik. I'm sure, when I do, she'll ask after you. I understand from your kind letters (forgive me for not replying, but you know how it is) that you are the proud father of two children. Of course I have not had the pleasure of meeting your wife but, please believe me, I am quite sure you will have been much happier with her than you could have ever been with poor Grace Lapraik.

Your sister, Isobel.

William had hoped Isobel would reply, thanking him for the money and answering his queries. Had Grace, indeed, ever asked after him? Had there been more dealings between Isobel and both the Lapraiks after he'd left?

But the next he heard of Isobel was two years later when the family lawyer informed him of her death. Like Uncle Robert, she died intestate. William considered returning to help arrange her funeral, and Lena encouraged him to do so. But it would have coincided with a key United Nations meeting in Geneva, so he let the lawyer deal with it all. Number 29 Bunnahabhain Road was sold quickly and at a fixed price to pay off Isobel's many debts. William considered for a while tracking down an address or phone number for Grace and Morag Lapraik, but this was in the early seventies – a crucial period in Namibia's quest for independence. The UN, after years of debate and pressure, finally decreed Pretoria's occupation of South-West Africa illegal and William's skills in political economy were in great demand for several years.

As time passed, he discovered that each individual little

Windhoek had its own dream, lighting up the dark Kalahari nights like so many little moons. Every man, woman and child had his or her own version of what the future held. On every street corner they spoke a different language, in each shop they sold you the trinkets of a different life. By accident William had ended up in a city that was the opposite of the one he was born and grew up in. Windhoek was a city of too many dreams. Glasgow, of too few.

In 1990, the new independent Republic of Namibia was finally proclaimed. William, at fifty-five years old, was invited to leave the tungsten business to take up a part-time position in the new government's Financial Planning Department in recognition of his services to the South-West Africa People's Organisation.

So here he now is, an elder statesman of a fledgling country; husband to a beautiful and loving wife, father to two upstanding children, grandfather to three beautiful examples of miscegenation. In good health, filling his time between meetings with fishing trips and rounds of golf and tending to his garden. His life is complete in ways he could never have imagined as a young man in the north. But last night, he made a phone call to Glasgow, took the first step in a six-thousand-mile journey back home.

He had vowed never to return. He'd left in anger and Africa had welcomed him warmly. He owes nothing to that grey old city of his childhood. Nor do they want him back there. Mrs Morag Simms, last night on the phone, almost begged him not to come. Last year's letter was a mistake, she said. She wasn't thinking straight. Wasn't that obvious from the letter? she said. She'd been ill; should never have contacted him in the first place.

But it felt too much like an opportunity, her letter coming out of the blue, despite the claptrap about ascensions and what have you. An invitation. Lena encouraged him, said he ought to go back, see the old place, look up old friends, get it out of his system. See if he can't now, with a lifetime's experience and wisdom under his belt, get a glimpse of the city his father thought so very wonderful.

On the telephone, Morag finally agreed to meet him — on the express condition that he did not attempt to contact her mother without her authorisation, which, she warned him, she may never give. That's fine. He's not going back to see Grace. Not in particular.

It's Saturday today and William goes out into the garden to do a spot of watering and pruning. The lechers next door are behaving themselves these days. Their daughter and little grandson are staying for a while, so the old couple keep themselves covered up and their hands to themselves. The minute the young family leave, they'll be up to their tricks again, peering at and pawing each other's crumbling bodies. It's happened before. Today, though, it's peaceful and William looks out over the plain towards Windhoek proper, feels a rush of pride for the city he helped bring together, make whole.

Six thousand miles, a disastrous love affair, forty years and the creation of a country to get to here. Time to go back, if only to measure the distance. Verify the outcome of his calculations. Couple of weeks. A month, maximum. Prove to himself he was right to leave. That, just as his father had invented his dream city, so in a way had William.

He sits in his deckchair, closes his eyes, smiles to himself at daft Morag Simms' fantasy of people rising up into the heavens. He drifts off into a half-sleep and dreams of Grace, naked, hanging in the sky, strands of silver hair glinting in the sun. She's ascending slowly, smiling, arms outstretched towards him.

2

FOUR

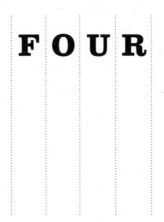

He'd been Cannibal ever since he was thirteen and had bitten a great lump out of his mother's face. Except he didn't, but felt it in his interests to let it be believed that he did. In reality it was a dog. One of the pack that graze and hunt in the savannas between the housing estates to the north of the city.

Elspeth'd been walking back from the shopping centre, took a short cut through the grasslands, stopped to sort out the messages that were tearing open the thin plastic bags. She checked first to see if the dogs were anywhere around the territory, but they can appear out of nowhere, these troops. She looked up and they'd ambushed her. About twelve of them, a burlesque of dwarves and giants, the wee ones with big ears, big ones with no tails, an atrocious miscegenation of stumpy legs, bandy bodies and teeth worn down to murderous spikes. They snarled and groaned *sotto voce*, Cannibal's mum just waiting, until one of them managed a crippled pounce and took a piece of her left cheek. The rest of the pride seemed content with that, and they all trotted off squintily. She didn't bother with the doctor's – she'd only been the once and'd left with a flea in her ear. The wound healed all right, no infection or anything, but the teeth-marks were clearly evident on her skin, and Cannibal saw his chance.

Cannibal's supposed biting of his own dear mother's face triggered a series of events which altered the geography of his life. In his third year in secondary, in 1995, he was removed in his own best interests from his childhood district, placed in an off-site care provision in the west of the city. Dudhope Road – some shambolic old wreck of a street. But Arran House, a home for children in need, was a big place, and Cannibal found himself surrounded for the first time in his life by shops and buses and people and trees, where all the streets looked different and the dogs were all tightly leashed. He had regular meals when he wanted them and, by the end of his second year in the institution, he and his friends had also taken up illegal part-time residence in an empty flat on the other side of the road.

Cannibal and his chums – Mags, Bubbles, Photofit and Koff – were enterprising youths, well known and even admired in the neighbourhood for their various money-making ventures. They ran for several months a car-washing service, later an indoor spring-cleaning service (supervised of course by the householder). They ran for nigh on a whole year a garden-tending business, until it ended, infamously, when it was discovered that all the while it had been a front for the cultivation of and trade in marijuana. It was Bubbles who spotted the parent plant in the back green of a little old lady's flat. The lady was very fond of the flowering annual, though found it hard to control and had no idea what it was. She was most pleased with the youngsters' tender care and scrupulous pruning of the plain but pretty bush. Before long half the ladies of the city's Golden Triangle of well-to-do households were maintaining enormous supplies of ganja. Many of them, including the old dear whom the Director referred to as their 'Guardian Angel' because she was supposed to have founded the place or something, and her daughter, argued long and hard on behalf of Cannibal and his friends when the police eventually came to call.

Cannibal was disappointed when the gardening business had to be closed down. In the area of the city he hailed from the only flowers around were daffodils. As a boy he had never really thought much about them, until his dad had made a surprising comment.

They'd been walking along one April day, and his dad had said,

—Fucken daffodils.

Cannibal had just been thinking they looked quite nice. But looking again, he could see what his father meant. There were millions of the things, huge perfectly rectangular banks of them, like they'd been brought in in giant trays and plonked down in the middle of the motorway that cut through the estate, or slap-bang in the middle of the grasslands. Specially delivered, once-a-year, large-cupped Sun Chariot and sweet-sweet Liberty Bell varieties: consolation for living on terrain where only pebble-dash and breeze-block grow naturally. The wild beasts of the vicinity made good use of the flowers, bedding down amongst them, daffies being perfect camouflage for their liver-and-dung-coloured markings.

—I hate fucken daffodils.

His dad lopped the head off one and kicked the roots of another to get his point across.

—Bastards, so they are.

This lesson from his father led to another key incident in Cannibal's journey from the north to the west of the city. On a late spring evening, past nine, a bleary band of light in the sky like a fluorescent tube, Cannibal took his father's cue and organised a full-scale attack on the central reservation yellow peril. He and his schoolfriends ran amok, whooping and sliding and kicking shit out of those blossom-blaring trumpets. The combat didn't overly tax them, given that the narcissi were already rotting with grey mould. Great clouds of petals and sepals and stamens soared into the air, turning orange in the fading light, floating down in shreds like confetti. Cannibal and his friends laid themselves down in the midst of it all, showered in pure ochre, the fragments of flowers covering them with a feather-light blanket of golden down. Later, Cannibal spoke of the experience often, remembering breathing gently in the fine daffodil dust and the silence.

The final straw, the head teacher had said. Taken together with a dysfunctional family background and negative attitudes in the classroom, Cannibal was referred by the child psychologist to Arran House, five miles across the city, several universes away. The people there – the adults – were even more alien than the ones he'd known at school. The Director a pure headcase, the Guardian Angel an old busybody who darted around at the speed of light, her big, fat daughter forever giving you big smiles that you could see right through and knew fine well she hated your guts. The psychologist a complete warmer. The other kids were all right, though.

After a week or so, they started taxiing him back every day to his old school – which hacked off the Heidie, watching the boy he wanted expelled hop in a taxi every afternoon to be chauffeured to a big house up west. Cannibal didn't mind being back north – so long as he could give his family a body-swerve. The bright, new estate of his birthright was hardly one of the worst in the city. Not like Pollok, where Bubbles came from, nor Mags's Castlemilk, Photofit's Queenslie, where half the windows are boarded up and the nightly ice-cream van's half-hour visit provides the only hub of conversation and clubbability. Cannibal's estate was a cut above. The city ring road links up a whole string of towns like Cannibal's, crags of quartz snapped off from the city proper like broken beads on a cheap necklace. A desirable enough location, relatively speaking, with a surprisingly high proportion of owner-occupiers, even though the architecture and interiors are exactly the same as in Queenslie, Castlemilk or Bubbles's Beirut of the North.

The bad thing about Cannibal's estate was the unnatural silence housed in so much concrete and brick. The misplaced tranquillity of a sleepy village where there should be noise and bustle and activity. Tens of thousands of people, and you never saw any of them out on the streets. Not what the planners had in mind, no doubt, for these new villages in the country.

The good thing was the surrounding hills. In the west, around Arran House, you can't see hills anywhere. But where Cannibal comes from there's wild land every which way, stretching out at the end of every street. Nobody ventured into it much but Cannibal used to wonder, every time he turned a corner, his footsteps ringing out solely in the silence, what lay out there. And sometimes he'd plan that one day he wouldn't turn the corner, but just keep on walking, walking, his steps echoing out beyond the concrete and tar until they became hushed and sumped in the permissible wetness and proper peace of the countryside.

Still, he was glad at the end of the day to get back west.

He had a lot going for him over here. The legends of his matricidal appetite and fearlessness in the face of savage botany had earned him a solid reputation; there were high jinks and capers to be had with his band of pals, and they even had their very own den to play in. A job too, all lined up. A big one this time, for Stoney Malone.

Stoney Malone was the Arran House clients' principal inward investor, furnishing the financial backing for most of their ventures, as well as providing a kind of minimum infrastructure and business know-how to help them make a success of their enterprises. Stoney'd help set the gardening service up, and the car-washing, and had seen Cannibal and his team's way clear to using the basement flat across the road. They generally only ever saw him at the back of Arran House, in the lane, in the shadows, instructing them to keep his name out of everything. He was useful, though, a powerhouse of ideas, always ready to make available little essential services. Like the leaflets he had printed out for them:

Cleans' A Whistle
Car-Washing and Valeting Service's
Family Car Soap 'n' Dry: £8.00
Plus Polish: £15.00
'All in under half an hour!'

And:

Gardenia's
Garden 'Make-Over' Service
Mowing, Weeding, Pruning, Raking,
Watering, Planting
'You name it – We Do it!!'
Price's On Request.

The young entrepreneurs would go around leafleting houses for a few days, then follow up a week later with personal calls. From time to time, Stoney would give them use of a mobile phone. He would collect all the money, and work out percentages and payments. All he charged in return was a levy of thirty per cent of takings.

Sometimes he charged more. Sometimes he liked the youngsters to pay him visits at his home. Play daddies. Once Cannibal, a bit of a favourite with Stoney, had to lie naked on the kitchen table while Stoney had his meal, in the scud too, eating with one hand, fondling Cannibal with the other. But it was all worth it in the end. Especially when Stoney Malone gave them the best news they could imagine – there was an empty basement flat across the way at number 17 Dudhope that he knew would not be occupied for some time. He OKed them breaking into it, making use of the place, so long as they kept a low profile. They could treat the place as their very own hideaway. There would be a price to pay for this luxury, naturally, and Stoney said he'd fill them in on the details in due course. Only Cannibal and Bubbles were allowed to open the flat up, though Photofit, Koff and Mags, as regular posse members, were given a free run of the place, and from time to time they all brought across from the home a few of their younger pals. There, they drank wine and cider bought on the proceeds of their various business ventures, or skinned up whenever one of the older graduates of Arran House passed by and shared. Or, less frequently, enjoyed the odd aerosol or PrittStick that Mags'd brought home from work placement. Between bouts and laughs and silent dances – a game they'd made up all on their own – they discussed the latest enterprises suggested by Stoney.

Mags was the devil's advocate, and very good at it she was too, coming up with all sorts of problems that were best ironed out before going public. Photofit didn't say much, but was a grafter and dependable. Bubbles cooked up wild schemes that would never see the light of day but which, in their sheer audacity, posed a constant threat to Cannibal's leadership. Bubbles, Cannibal said, thought he was the dog's bollocks. But what caused the most heated debate of all was, after a few days of enjoying the flat, Stoney told them the plan. Their mission was to torch their lovely new basement den.

Bubbles – a true man of action – was for executing Stoney's wishes at the earliest opportunity. Cannibal and Mags were for delaying as long as possible. Stoney had been abnormally flexible over this commission, stating only that he would be totally incommunicado with all the Arran inmates for precisely two months, at the end of which time, the second week of March, he wanted the job completed. Not long after, he would reappear with an unspecified amount of poppy to divvy out among the gang. Cannibal's and Mags's objection to immediate action, when there was no call for it, was that once the place was torched, as per Stoney's requirements, they'd lose their little private gaff, mess as it was, and thus have no escape from the regimented life of Arran House any more.

Eventually, Cannibal exercised his veto. They would wait until the last possible moment before acting on Stoney's instructions to burn the basement of number 17 to the ground. They had six whole weeks in which to enjoy the comparative warmth and social possibilities of the unfurnished flat. Ideal for a high-spirited group of youngsters who were always on the go but could never find enough places to go *to*. They darted here and there, always on the lookout for adventures. As kids will. Moving in a haphazard motion around the city, Mags getting breathless along Dumbarton Road, veering off left, right, ending up in the city centre, forever putting off the moment to stop somewhere, nowhere, for no reason, as long as possible. They'd cut up right, down left and were spotted in the oddest places: the Govan side of the old quays along the river; Mugdock (a good three-hour walk from the west end, in the countryside); Victoria Park, where they sat beside the boat pond, and paddled their feet and ankles down through the crisp pokes and Coke tins and used condoms into the water. There they'd sit and chat and joke, watching pond-skater bugs dart expertly through the clabber and clat in perfectly straight lines, crisscrossing each other without accident in a crazed, angular dance.

Gaining entry to the gaff allowed the group of friends some respite from their endless toing and froing, and they happily set up part-time home amongst the old cardboard boxes and peeling wallpaper and linoleum. They brought an old kettle over from Arran House, there were still old chipped cups in the cupboard, and the electricity and the water had never been turned off. So they could have cups of tea or make Cup a Soup or Pot Noodles, and sit around. From time to time Bubbles would bring some of the younger girls from the home over and he and Photofit could play around with them, Mags looking on. The odd night they stayed out – skipping out after lights out and truanting until early morning, creeping back through the windows of Arran House before breakfast. On such nocturnal adventures Mags used to let Cannibal cuddy up beside her under the blankets pinched from the home. Then the pair of them would giggle and laugh together and Cannibal'd tell her that she'd got herself clinically obese on purpose, just to keep him at bay. Mags'd laugh and tell him that he sounded like one of the daft child psychologists over at Arran.

On days when all or one of them decided not to take

their taxis to school, the den provided a place to pass the time of day. All in all, they agreed, the gaff was a good thing. Kept them off the streets and out of trouble. Once torched, it would be the end of an era.

For Cannibal, Mags, Photofit and Koff, much as the prospect of such a big bonfire excited them, the concomitant prospect of rendering themselves gaffless restrained them. Bubbles, though, was especially fond of the smell of burning and liked to play with matches, and there remained throughout the weeks of waiting the possibility that he'd just jump straight up and do it now. Quite apart from the luxury the empty flat afforded them, Cannibal was aware that the operation needed to be planned in military detail. Local residents had seen them come and go. Most of the time the five tried to enter and exit discreetly, but sometimes they were caught out, and at other times events overtook them and they made quite a spectacle of themselves.

Only a week or so after Stoney had given the order for the burning – no doubt an insurance scam of some sort on behalf of the owner – they had all had a field day. Mags had brought back an industrial-size refill canister of liquid paper, Bubbles had procured a fistful of various undenominated capsules of bright and varying colours from an Arran graduate, and Koff had managed to pinch two bottles of Thunderbird wine in Safeway. The five of them entered the flat in conspicuous disarray. Photofit singing 'The Fields of Athenry' at the top of his voice; Mags stopping outside the close for a quick pee (reasonable enough seeing as how the lavatory inside didn't work and the pan was already full to overflowing). Koff on his hands and knees screaming as usual fuckofukofkofkoff. Cannibal not really helping much by yelling at everyone to keep the racket down.

Only Bubbles – oddly, him being generally the most

vocal and least concerned about neighbours or noise pollution – kept quiet and seemed comparatively sober. Once inside they broke the silence vow of their Silent Dance and jumped around with the bottles of wine and rolled against the walls at full volume, shouting and singing and laughing. Then, tired out, they realised how cold it was inside the gaff and set about building a small campfire, carefully dismantling what was left of the old kitchen units for firewood. But it turned out to be more fun to do the dismantling uncarefully, and soon they began ripping rickety drawers into pieces, tearing cupboard doors to bits. Bubbles, astoundingly, stood back from all this, then suddenly pulled off an old brass handle from a drawer and sent it flying through the kitchen window. Which defeated the original purpose of the exercise – to heat themselves up. Bubbles, however, was extraordinarily pleased with himself.

The locals complained to Arran House, of course. The family upstairs, whose daughter was seriously ill, had called the police on the night of the disturbance. But the posse had their alibis sorted out, and there was nothing eventually that either the police or the management of the home could do about the incident. Bubbles took the surprising and unilateral step of volunteering to board up the kitchen window himself – even though he swore on his mother's life that the breaking of it had nothing to do with him. The friends waited for a respectable five days before breaking down the back door again and carrying on with life as before. Bubbles regularly checked his handiwork on the kitchen window, pleased with his newly acquired DIY skills.

Once back inside again, Cannibal realised the folly of their actions. When the place was eventually torched, it'd be too obvious who'd done it. Not a problem for Bubbles or Photofit or even Mags, who hoped that it might lead to a better placement, somewhere in the countryside maybe, and that would make a change. Cannibal was more realistic, feared they might end up somewhere far worse than Arran House.

—Like where? Bubbles sneered.

—Like that place where everyone's forever stringing themselves up.

—So? Bunch of shiters.

But Cannibal knew it was essential that they distance themselves from the eventual burning of the flat. That although people round about knew they'd been squatting in it, there must be nothing that would necessarily connect them with the arson. They could perhaps, after the event, suggest it was the handiwork of ex-Arran boys, or perhaps younger pupils who were jealous of the hang-out, and who'd tried to oust them. They wouldn't have to name names, just hint at who they might have been. That way they might have to take the rap for breaking and entering, but not for arson. Bubbles proposed that they should inflict a few minor burns on themselves, to prove that they had been innocent victims. He was disappointed when the others decided it'd be better that they claim they were nowhere near the place the day it got burnt down.

All of the inmates of Arran House were aware of the power of suggestion. Hints, half-truths, rumours were the lingua franca of their world. The idea that the eventual fire could have been caused by vague outsiders was perfectly credible. There were indeed Arran House graduates who turned up from time to time, usually for no particular reason. Somewhere to go. As did a whole host of other teenagers and early twentysomethings from the local schools and even from the fine, solid houses up in the Golden Triangle. Arran House acted as a kind of hub, a centre for gung-ho kids in search of adventure and new chums. People hung out there for all sorts of reasons: because they had a job wanting done, or were hoping that someone would invite them in on a scam. Or for potential sex, or just for someone to talk to, or some place to be. Or they were looking for information which they knew would be false, but false information's better than none.

They'd hang around and tell you what they'd been up to. The fights they'd been in, the drugs they'd dealt, the detox they'd been through, the women they'd had. All of which may have been half-true, or half of it completely true but, either way, you never knew which half. And Bubbles and Photofit and Cannibal would talk right back, exaggerating Stoney Malone stories and business profits and goings-on in Arran House. Everyone compared notes about parties and raves they'd never been to. It was generally believed that they were the sort of people who went to such things, though everyone knew that raves were really for the kids from the semis and big Victorian flats down the road. Few of even the ex-clients had the gear or the money to gain admission to such events, and they found they were seldom invited to parties.

The social workers and community police and carers dealt in this misty world all the time – inaccurate personal profiles and case histories, details of events which may never have taken place and virtually no information on incidents that most certainly *had* taken place. It would be easy enough, Cannibal reckoned, to fudge the issue of the gaff and its torching. The rule is: don't deny all knowledge of everything, know just enough and give hints in the wrong direction. That way nothing would ever happen, and nothing happening's the way everyone likes it. Except maybe for Bubbles.

With about three weeks to go before the date of the

kindling of 17 Dudhope Road, Cannibal came up with the blueprint for the action plan. The central plank of the plan was that they all change their image, an idea Cannibal'd got, he said, from something Mags had once told him.

—Mind that Paki girl? he said when she and he and Photofit and Koff and Bubbles were all assembled. —What she said about the genies.

—Jinns, Mags corrected him.

—Paki bogeymen.

—According to Nadjme, they're everywhere.

Cannibal insisted on retelling Mags's story himself.

—Millions of them, a whole world of them, living here, all around us, except we can't see them and they can't see us. They go about their business and we go about ours, in the same streets, houses, shops, everything. So, like, there's the guy behind the shop counter that serves us, and there's another jinn one there at the same time, serving his jinn customers. Except we don't see them and they don't see us. Just, every now and then, something happens, and we appear to them or they appear to us, or whatever. Some kind of breakthrough. But most of the time, we're all in it together but we don't know each other's there.

—Fucksakes. Bubbles was becoming impatient. —What's a wee Paki lassie's mince got to do with us changing our image?

Cannibal replies: —That's what hanging out around here's like. The natives are everywhere, you see them every day in the street, rub shoulders with them, bump into them, crash out in their gardens or set up your den in their basements.

Then he turns to face Bubbles directly and asks: —How long you been here now, Bubbles?

—Two year, off and on.

—Well you ever heard one single conversation between

these people round here? I mean you see them talking to each other, see their lips moving and that, but can you remember one single word any of them's ever said? Apart from telling you to stop that, or beat it, or that they're going to phone the police? It's like they're not really there, yes?

Bubbles says: —Suppose. But what's that got to do with the price of jellies?

—So that's how we are to them, says Cannibal.

—They can't tell us apart. Come the night of the big bonfire all they'll be able to remember was that there was one guy with lanky hair, one fat cow in a minging anorak, one ginger guy that wears the same T-shirt every day of the week. Change any wee thing about the way we look and they'll never be able to identify us.

Dissent in dress is frowned upon by the Arranites. Not long after he had come to the institution, Cannibal had watched Bubbles accosting a perfect stranger in the street. The man was wearing a fedora hat, which, despite it being a pouring wet day, annoyed Bubbles. He drummed up a group of his colleagues. All of them, except Cannibal, hair cropped, trainer laces dragging through puddles, flimsy wet T-shirts, the whole gear like scars they're out to avenge.

Bubbles, rain running down his nose, led them to the unsuspecting hat-wearer and said simply to him,

—Cunt.

The incident would have blown over if only the hat man hadn't looked at the band of drenched and drookit kids and retorted,

—Maybe. But at least I'm not a stupid cunt.

Thereafter, they identified his car, trashed it; identified his house on Patrick Brae, smashed his windows, and generally made a nuisance of themselves to the man and his family.

Cannibal had to spell it out: with the simplest of changes in their garb and hairstyles, no potential witness would ever be able to identify them. The idea didn't go down well, except with Photofit, who yearned for the opportunity to change himself and was unique amongst the friends in considering that change was possible.

—No point in you doing it, Photie, Cannibal said. —No matter what you do to yourself you'll always fit some description or other. Hence your name.

—Yeah, how come you gave us that name by the way? Photofit was sullen.

—Quite simply because you look like several different people stuck together. Nothing goes. Your nose is the wrong nose for your face, your face the wrong face for the rest of you. Your arms are short, your legs are long and your body looks like two different bodies glued together in the middle. Whoever's got the lower part that goes with the top must be hung like a horse. You've ended up with the useless bits. Result is that you look like everyone at the same time. You're unique, Photie. We want you to stay that way.

Despite the indifference of his troops to his suggestion, Cannibal decided that he himself would play safe and set about changing his appearance. He cut his long hair. Then, across the way in Arran House, he sifted through the clothes his mother had put in there for him when he'd first arrived and that he'd never worn. He picked out an old jumper she had knitted for him years back. It was a bit tight but it would do. And a leather jacket she'd bought second-hand, the far end of Argyll Street, and he'd always hated, but now that he looked at it again it didn't seem so bad.

Cannibal began the transformation of his physical self one week before the appointed date for the torching of the flat. In the intervening week, Mags and Bubbles and the rest more or less lost sight of him. He didn't come round to the basement flat, attended school faithfully for the entire week, sending the taxi away and walking home each evening to Arran House, arriving back late. He was on his best behaviour, taking his meals at the set times, then disappearing off for a walk or up to his room until lights out. He checked in with Mags on a daily basis, but only to make sure that Bubbles wasn't taking things into his own hands and planning on burning the gaff down without him.

In fact, Bubbles *was* practising his incendiary skills. He set alight every window sash in the home so that no window could be opened, and all that week everyone was sweating with the heat pumped out by the ancient oil radiators. He bought a box of bangers half price from the corner shop, most of them damp and done, left over from Guy Fawkes, and invented a little game, 'I Spy, Through a Hole in the Wall'. Promising the youngest intake of pupils all manner of goodies and delights, he got them to peek through the holes between the bricks in the back wall while he, on the other side, lit little blue tapers. Bang. It frustrated Bubbles that not one of his bangers had managed to blow a whole eye right out, clean.

Cannibal declined to deal with him directly but passed messages, via Photofit and Mags, that Bubbles might as well advertise in the national press that he was going to be an arsonist in the near future. Bubbles passed messages back, asking if Cannibal was getting cold feet, and if so then Bubbles had the means to warm them up for him. Far from chickening out, however, Cannibal was becoming increasingly excited by the prospect of the adventure, and remained determined that he would be the strategist behind it.

The torching of the basement was to be the rekindling

of Cannibal's life. Everything would be different after-wards. Ironic that the things you don't do, like bite your own mother's face, give you fame and a start in life, whereas something that you would actually do – burn down a west end tenement flat – no one could know about. Bubbles and Photofit would tell everyone it was them, but no one would believe them. Cannibal hoped that precisely by staying tight-lipped, everyone would suspect that he was the hero of the hour.

Cannibal had made a decision early in life, in the first days or weeks of secondary school. He came from a steady enough but deadly dull family. He had three sisters (the eldest, a year younger than Cannibal, had visited him once or twice at Arran House) all of them healthy, young, straightforward girls who couldn't for the life of them understand what went on in their big brother's head. As with most of Cannibal's classmates, there's conflicting evidence of any real trouble at home, with only vague assertions of 'dysfunctional family' peppered around his various files. His father was usually in full-time employ-ment, and had little history of drunkenness and violence.

Cannibal had gone up to the big school in the company of a few friends from the good side of the estate, all neat uniforms and patted-down hair. They were given a rough time by some of the boys, so Cannibal made a quick calcu-lation. He could risk life and limb, and at the same time bore himself to death, by remaining loyal to his primary school friends, or turn poacher and live a more interesting life. He chose the latter, and tried to impress the more rough and tumble lads. For all of the first year and most of the second he was little more than tolerated by these livelier and higher-spirited boys. Then he hit the jackpot, claiming responsibility for the teeth-marks on his mother's face. One year later he is proudly deemed disturbed, without ever actually having done anything except tear up a few daffodils.

After being sent to Arran House, Cannibal never once went back to see his family. He managed to win fiscal support for this decision by hinting at potential violence were he to return. However, he requested his taxi driver, at the end of the school day, to make a daily detour down his old street. No one, he thought, would expect to see him in a taxi, so there was little risk of being spotted. One day, he'd think to himself, he'd go in. See the old dears and Leigh-Anne and Natasha and Lisa. But not yet. Not until after the fire. Until he'd sorted himself out. Then he'd drop the name Cannibal. Assume another. He'd never go back to the housing estate for good, of course. How could you go back to a place that consisted of nothing but streets? Streets you walked down, hoping to come across something, and you never did. Streets and houses and flanks of daffodils. Built on open, hopeful green-field sites, and in their very construction burying the fields, and along with them, the hope. The construction of a grey desert, great craggy dunes with windows in them. Not even a real desert like they'd have in Africa or someplace, dangerous and wild and open, but a desert with a thousand frontiers. Streets upon streets upon streets, each one of them yet another boundary, an end, a closure.

Maybe he'd go to London like all the Arran ex-clients said they did but hadn't. Or up north. Or be an actor. Tell everyone he was from the worst part of Queenslie or Pollok. Or Granton maybe, or Wester Hailes. He could mimic the east coast accent no bother. More romantic places altogether. He could exaggerate his record: theft, GBH, arson of course. They liked that kind of thing, people who employ actors. He thinks about it, looking out through the window of his taxi. Looking back over the grey little houses, getting smaller in the distance, and at the big empty hills behind them, getting bigger, emptier.

They'd light the fire in the afternoon. It was decided. Bubbles wanted to do it at night, for the sheer romance and pyrotechnical display of it, but Cannibal reckoned the safest thing would be to do it in the light of day. The majority of the tenants in the building itself and on either side of it were usually out during the day. Cannibal knew their schedules well: a couple of months previously he had spent two entire weeks, on Stoney Malone's request – just previous to a series of break-ins – spying from the vantage point of his upstairs bedroom window, which overlooked the tenements opposite, noting down to the nearest quarter-hour when the residents of those three closes left their flats and when they returned.

The process was dogged by a girl in the first-storey flat above the basement across the way, who must've been off on the sick 'cause she was always sitting at the big bay window peering out into everybody's business. Instead of sitting in an armchair, headphones on, making his notes comfortably like he'd planned, Cannibal had to crouch on the floor, popping up every couple of minutes. Probably he needn't have bothered – he was invisible to her, like they all were to everyone round here, like the Paki jinns. But then, a stroke of luck. For the last few days before the appointed torching, the lassie disappeared. Cannibal checked round the back of the tenement and, right enough, after a few hours' wait, she appeared in her dressing gown at one of the bedroom windows. Must've taken to her bed, and so long as she didn't get better in the next couple of days, they'd be all right. By the look of her, pure white and knackered-looking, she'd be in her scratcher for ages.

The middle of the afternoon was undoubtedly the safest

time. The students in the top flat of number 17 were out all day; below them, a guy living alone who went out to work and never came back till about five; across from him the nosy sick girl, and her family who were also out all day. Next door, down towards Arran House, there were a couple of families – after lunch until about four they were all out at school or work or whatever. Across the way, a flashy bint and a bunch of blacks. All out during daylight hours. All that remained was to plan out the ignition of the fire itself.

There was no need for complicated deceptions. No need to make it look accidental, a cigarette or gas stove fire. It would be obvious that the fire was deliberate no matter what they did. So long as they, or anyone connected to Stoney, weren't in the frame. At the appointed hour – 3.15 p.m. – they would simply sneak quietly in, making sure they weren't noticed, bundle up the old mattresses, papers, debris, break a few Bic lighters and perhaps some petrol if they could siphon a car somewhere. Chuck a few matches and scarper.

Stoney had commissioned a decent fire that would do some damage, but not too huge that would spread and cause significant structural harm. Certainly not big enough to affect the conjoining flats. They therefore decided to start the fire in the kitchen, which was in the corner of the house, and leave the door and main door open so that the smoke would escape and be seen quickly. On the day in question, they would wear gloves so that no fresh finger-prints could be found. Cannibal imposed a ban on re-enter-ing the place from the Sunday afternoon. They would later state that, yes, they had been in the flat the previous morning, but had not returned. As for alibis, Bubbles had already persuaded six of the third and fourth years to skip school the following day, then they could testify that they'd been with Bubbles and Cannibal and Mags and Photofit all afternoon down the pond in Victoria Park.

On the appointed day, the gang of friends met up secretly in a clump of trees in the lane behind Arran House. The rest all laughed when they saw Cannibal: he'd done a wizard job of disguising himself. Hair cut right into the bone, the knitted jersey and leather jacket too wee for him. He looked younger, lighter. But healthy. You really noticed his bright, green eyes, his smooth skin, no hint of a beard yet. He looked like a real leader. Every bit the Boy King. Alexander going into his first battle. Cannibal the Hannibal.

They crept the long way round to the den. Keeping to the side streets, then up the lane that ran behind the shops, in through the back gate to the common green, staying close to the walls and in amongst the overgrowth, like secret service agents camouflaged in the unkempt grasses and weeds and bushes. Then in the back close door, and into the flat. They had already, the previous afternoon, built a hill of bedclothes, cereal boxes, teabags (Bubbles swore they burnt slow and long), old shoes, all balanced on two old mattresses.

Really, the pyre was just a heap of old junk, but the five friends were very proud of it. It pleased them, and they stood around admiring its dappled ochres and damp browns. It looked understated, modest, but as if it knew itself what it was about to achieve. It was higgledy-piggledy, yet gave the impression of having some kind of internal order. Like the shoe that stuck upwards, or the torn canvas of the mattress corner, the flattened cardboard box, none if it looking like it'd just been thrown on any old way, but like they'd constructed it, item by item, to create this aesthetic whole. And they liked the idea that later that day, or tomorrow, when the firemen had put out the blaze, there it still would be, in the middle of the room, this same shape. Reduced in size and blackened, smouldering through the water, but still with the same edges jutting out, still their own work.

Cannibal allowed Bubbles to finish it off by adding the cocktail of flammable liquids they'd been storing next to it. Near-empty aerosols of insecticides, paint stripper, anything they found in local bins – none of it, under Cannibal's instructions, from Arran House. Over this, Bubbles poured about a half-pint of petrol they'd manage to siphon off from an old motorbike in a driveway. Then he smashed a few fifty-pence lighters with a crowbar, threw them on too. Finally, what was left of the box of bangers he'd bought. Photofit stepped forward and sprinkled on a few more cheap lighters, whole.

Without saying a word, they all moved as one. Slowly, to perform their own ritual dance before the spark was added. Cannibal, scrabbling around in the loamy earth, hands stiffly down at his sides, like he was doing some backwater country dance. Mags rotating around the walls, a big green cylinder rolling round and round, her already filthy anorak getting encrusted with the damp mire. Koff pogoing, Photofit waving his arms around, and doing little Latin-like shuffles with his feet, laughing silently. The Silent Dance.

If anyone were to witness this strange ritual they'd think the dancers were all out of it. In fact, they had none of them drunk alcohol that day, nor taken any other substance. Mags maintained that the five of them tended anyway to limit themselves to blow and eggs and alcohol, jellies, Eve, the odd treat in a flake of snow. Cannibal was of the opinion that the authorities, more than just turning a blind eye to scag being made available in the areas they came from and the institutions they were sent to, actively encouraged it, and he was therefore dead against its use. Mags reckoned he was really just a scaredy-cat about needles.

There were only two rules to the dance: complete silence for the duration, and Bubbles was the only legitimate MC. The dance pre-existed Cannibal's arrival at Arran House, and was handed down to Bubbles to pass on to the next generation. Bubbles is always in the middle. In this case, nearest to the pyre. He starts with sit-ups, and then goes into a kind of syncopated training circuit, a clue perhaps to the Dance's origin, a step aerobics class somewhere, taking off his shirt as they reach the climax. When Mags's wall-roll takes her near to him, she stops, stoops, runs her hand over his torso, then retreats to the wall, continues rotating.

How long the Dance lasts depends on Bubbles. He's stretched it out for a couple of hours in the past till everyone's wilting, tiredness taking the hush out of their steps, Mags thumping against the wall, Koff hopping, half-hearted, Photofit scuffing the earth. The last movement of the Dance is signalled by a high-pitched screech from Bubbles. Then at regular intervals he calls again, each time a lower note and the Dance is over when he descends to a long, continuous bass hum. They all slump where they are, exhausted but calm.

On this occasion, in anticipation of holy fire, Bubbles speeds the process up until he's doing sit-ups and press-ups at a superhuman rate, the rest bouncing and rolling manically, trying to keep up. He screeches early – and more quietly, so as not to alert neighbours or passers-by outside – and descends to his bass hum, more of a gurgle really, the excitement having produced an excess of phlegm in his throat. The dance is over with in under seven minutes. Now, without a word being exchanged, Bubbles steps forward with his box of matches, and sets each corner of their debris sculpture alight. They all watch, motionless, as the dampness fights with the dribbles of lighter fuel, and the smoke begins to thicken. They turn their attention to Cannibal, expecting some kind of homily from their leader.

—When volcanoes erupt they destroy everything. Everything. But then after a while. A few years maybe. Maybe a few hundred, or thousand, things that'd never grown there before, start to. Weird, new things. Plants and trees and animals that had never been seen or thought of before, impossible to describe, begin to appear . . .

He wanted to say more, searched for the words in the now smoking pyre, and in the eyes of his friends. But they were happy with what he had said already, and all nodded gravely. So Cannibal cast his eyes downward. The others followed his example. Then he began to shuffle backwards away from the sooty flames towards the door. Mags and Photofit and Koff did likewise. But Bubbles stood his ground. He stared into the fire, and then he turned to Cannibal, holding his gaze firmly, and smiled.

—Know what? says Bubbles in a quiet voice.

—I've never lit an illegal fire in my life. Until the window cords last week there.

This was Big News. It was always understood that Bubbles'd been expelled from various schools as a result of persistent destructive activity. It had also always been assumed that some of those activities involved fire – given the boy's love for that most powerful of elements. Bubbles had always shown a particular affinity with all things incendiary, and his glee at the prospect of torching the gaff led everyone to believe that he had the necessary skills and experience for tackling the job professionally.

In fairness, though, it was not arson that had led to his

referral to Arran House, but the theft of a 42B bra from C&A. The Children's Panel wanted to know why he had attempted to steal that particular article and Bubbles became quite upset at the suggestion that he'd intended wearing it, claiming he'd only stolen it at his mother's behest. Mrs Bubbles confirmed this, though insisted she'd meant for him to buy it, given him the money, but he'd spent it on dog biscuits. Pursuing this line of enquiry, the Children's Panel discovered that there is no dog in the Bubbles family home, and the proceedings ended in some confusion. It was decided nevertheless that this incident, taken together with his school record and past petty crimes, earned him a place in Arran House. Janice Baird, the psychologist attached to Arran House, escorted Bubbles and his mother to her car to run them home, whereupon Bubbles produces a brown paper bag with dog biscuits and begins crunching them. Janice attempted to enlist the mother's support to get him to stop, but Bubbles's mother took the dog biscuits from him and eats them herself, offering the biscuits to Janice to try. To this day Bubbles enjoys an occasional bag of Winalot – an obstacle, together with the commonly held opinion that he is well on his way to becoming a fully fledged violent sociopath, every time his release back into the community is discussed.

Photofit, Mags, Koff and Cannibal looked at him in disbelief, while the smoke thickened. Bubbles goes on to confess that not only has he never started a fire, but in fact he's never been in a fight of any great seriousness – though each of them in that simmering room had seen Bubbles in action often enough. As well as the fedora-wearer, he had waged a campaign of terror, quite arbitrarily, against a local, shy-looking lad who lived in a detached house at the back of Arran, had enlisted their and others' active service in throwing bottles at him, ambushing him in the street, until finally the family moved away, declining the police's offer to press charges, for fear of a heightened campaign of revenge. Presumably, though, for Bubbles it was all a matter of scale and such skirmishes did not register.

Bubbles then turns to Photofit and says, —What about you, Photie?

Bubbles was a master of the unexpected. He had turned a moment of communion into one of confession, as if the fire they had started could somehow cleanse them. That it would not leap into flame until the past had been purged and truth was made victorious.

—I'm just here because I don't fit in anywhere else.

—What about the shoplifting?

Bubbles put him under pressure.

—Me? Nah.

In reality, Photofit had indeed had a short but successful career in audacious blagging, always of items of little or no use to him. After his Panel hearing, he led them to a muddy burn, a tributary of the Clyde, that ran through the back of the scheme where he lived. The smouldering pyre he and his friends were standing before now was a mere hillock in comparison to the mountain of drenched bookcases, hairdriers, rolls of wallpaper, telephones, computer hardware and software, bags of nappies and electric guitars they found there.

Photofit was caught up in Bubbles's moment. He used the rule he normally reserved for adults: tell them what they want to hear. Anything else is pointless. Bubbles was assuming the role of adult. Authority. So far Cannibal had been the strategist, but now it was Bubbles who was taking charge.

—Mags?

Mags is classic: abused, violent home, rejected by peers, the lot. Gift of a case, really.

—They put a court order on me for my own protection.

Bubbles was tickled pink at the idea.

—Christ. And they put you in Arran for *safe keeping*?

Mags protested: —Course, it's a load of shite. I was just fed up at school, that's all.

—How about you, Koff?

The friends all smiled at the look of confusion on Koff's face. Not the brightest of boys, Koff was confused as to how the world around him worked. After spending the lion's share of his first three years at school under his desk, squealing at people to fuck off, he was referred to Janice Baird, whereupon he took off his shoes and asked her if she could also help with a verruca on his foot. To Koff, psychologists, social workers, doctors are all the same: if you've got a suit and a briefcase and ask questions about people's home lives, presumably you know about verrucas too, or can pull a tooth.

—Fuckoffuckoff.

Cannibal didn't wait to be asked. It wasn't a big deal anyway. He didn't feel the need to confess, or the need to resist. Sometimes denial merely serves to confirm the act being denied. When Bubbles turned to him, staring expectantly, he decided to play along with the game. It made no difference now anyway – his past was about to go up in smoke with the mattresses and bangers.

—Never bit anyone in my life.

The reaction was bigger than he'd bargained for. Mags and Photofit stared at him, open-mouthed. Bubbles smiled. His wet, saliva-drenched grin was full of pleasure and Cannibal understood he'd been tricked. Bubbles'd planned this moment. His coup. It'd never occurred to Cannibal that Bubbles had a planning brain cell in his head. Cannibal in the past had had to outdo violent outbursts from Bubbles, top him in the madness stakes. He'd assumed it would always be like that. So long as he was on his guard and ready to outwit Bubbles, he'd retain the leadership of this particular little group of Arranites. But cool, logical preparation he had not been ready for.

—See, the difference is, Canny, we're all lying *now*. But you've been lying all along.

Bubbles turned to the posse for validation of this assertion, and they all stared accusingly at Cannibal. Lying, of course, was not the issue. There were no lies amongst the clients of Arran House. How can there be lies when there is no fixed truth?

—Everyone knows I'm a mental bastard, Bubbles said.

Cannibal had played his cards wrong, that's all. Leadership was about knowing how to react at precise moments. He should have kept the myth of his cannibalism going until after the fire had scorched their den. He had lost the moment.

The flames began to climb. Cannibal stepped back up to the fire, stood as close as the smoke and heat would allow.

—This is no time for arguments.

—Who's arguing?

—Remember now, everyone. All of you be back at Arran in ten minutes.

—What if we don't? You going to bite us?

Bubbles laughed, then Cannibal heard the rest of them chiming in. He felt a rush of anger. Then he felt the loss of the heat from the fire, and then a breeze wafting coolly over his body. He felt his limbs move, and it was as if he was flying, as if his legs were being lifted off the ground by some silent but hungry power. He felt the roof of his mouth dry and corrugated, his cheeks swelling, forced outwards by some foreign body, his incisors pushed down against a hard, taut surface, bursting through that surface and sinking into soft, wet moistness. Bubbles's yell signalled what had happened, and Cannibal, revolted, pulled his lips and teeth away from the ginger bristle and red pustules on Bubbles's cheek.

Bubbles screamed some words at him that Cannibal couldn't make out, and Koff and Photofit were shouting something too. And then they weren't there any more. Mags screaming somewhere in the distance. Cannibal was alone, he and his pyre, smoking blackly now, and the door of the kitchen was locked. He remembered the instructions on the home wall about what to do in case of fire, and got down on his belly, slithered towards the window. Before he got there he remembered Bubbles's handiwork at boarding it up, and was impressed with the forward planning and patience. He clambered up anyway on the old china Belfast sink, tried sucking the air in through the cracks in Bubbles's handiwork, hammered away at the boards. But they wouldn't budge. He sat inside the huge sink, feeling guilty that he wasn't panicking enough.

There was a deadly silence in the room now. The fire glowed scorchingly but made no noise. The smoke was thickening but as yet wasn't choking him. He sat and tried to think of what to do, and came quickly to the conclusion that there was nothing whatsoever he could do. He looked at the fire and judged that it was beyond putting out quickly. Bubbles'd even had the forethought to turn the water off. So he just sat there in his deep sink, surprised that he wasn't thinking of anything at all.

A godalmighty explosion thunderclapped around the room and tugged him out of his torpor. He expected the fire, properly ignited now, would swallow up the room and him with it, waited for the great tongues of demonic flames to lick out at him. But the pyre smouldered and glowed as before, and Cannibal realised the explosion had just been one of Bubbles's bangers going off. There was silence again, a quietness when there should have been noise that made him think of his street, his house, his sisters and dad, his mother, and he would have liked to have left a note for her, but even if he had a pen or pencil or paper, the note too would get eaten up in the flames.

In the silence he could hear his own breathing, the way he did when he'd laid down amongst the daffodils one night a long time ago. Then, a banging somewhere. On the ceiling. Coming from the flat above. The lassie, the sick lassie, it must be her. The smoke must be going up through her floorboards. Probably, all she could do was smell some faint smoke and she was thinking there was a group of them down there with a wee controlled fire that they were cooking sausages on or the like. She'd have no idea that the place was a smouldering wreck, was about to go up in flames any minute now. Or maybe the smoke was thick up there too, and she was trapped in bed or whatever, couldn't get out.

Cannibal climbed back out of his sink, pulled a charred brush from out of the pyre, pulled himself back up on to the sink, precariously balanced a foot on either side of the china sides and managed to strike the ceiling above, over and over again, as hard as he could without falling off his perch.

—Get out of there! Get out, for Chrissakes!

Maybe the place really would go up in a big, massive explosion and take the girl upstairs with it, as well as him. Or perhaps she was too sick to get out of the house. Christ knows, she looked like shit the other day. It wasn't that Cannibal felt a huge urge to save the unknown lassie. He didn't even much like her, the way she kept nosying into everybody's business and staring out her window. But if he did get out of here, he didn't want done for Murder One, like they do on the telly. The whole point of the exercise was to get the hell out of Dudhope and homes and places they locked you up. Then again, if the fire *did* do for him, then Bubbles would go down for double murder if the lassie upstairs got burnt alive too. It wasn't fair, though. She had nothing to do with them; they had nothing to do with her. Like the jinns, they lived in separate worlds. What if Natasha or Leigh-Anne or Lisa got caught up in somebody else's fire? Cannibal tried to get back up on the sink again. Had to warn her. Had to shout up, warn the sick, nosy slag.

But the smoke was beginning to get to him. He fell down off the sink. Kept trying to scream up but his throat had packed in on him. Could feel his lips moving, could feel the effort of pumping air up from his lungs into his throat, but no sound came out. The silence was complete. No crackling, no screaming. He wondered if he had gone deaf, for the burning room should've been thundering, cracking. Next thing, he couldn't see either. And he felt again that he was being picked up and floating through air, presumed that he must be falling.

—Ma?
—You OK?
Wasn't his mother, it was Mags. Cannibal looked round, he was out in the close, the smoke from the fire bellowing out of the back door of the basement flat. He lay back on the cool, cold stone of the close floor. He felt like a soldier who'd been pulled out of battle by a comrade. Two Little Boys, except Mags was a girl and he was decked out in a Glasgow tenement close, not the Fair Fields of France, his lungs feeling like they'd been stretched out on a washboard

and scrubbed with steel wire. He was trying to remember something that he had to do. The lassie upstairs. The soldier still had his mission to complete. He tried to get up on to his feet.

—What're you doing?

—Help me up the stair.

He managed to find his way to the banister and began heaving himself up the shallow steps, Mags following him, yelling at him to stop. He got halfway up, and tried shouting.

—Get out of that flat there.

His voice was working again, but there was no strength in it. Still, he kept doing his best to shout. The door above him opened and the girl, the sick lassie, came out on to the landing.

—Get out, he wheezed.

—What's happened down there?

She curled her lip at Cannibal and Mags.

—Daft bastards. You'll have us all burnt. Don't you care about anyone? Anything? Ruin everything you touch.

Then she turned to go inside while Mags led Cannibal back downstairs.

—Just you wait till I get the fire brigade.

—Hope you die, said Mags, and the sick girl just looked at her, pale and scared and tearful. Cannibal pulled Mags down the close towards the daylight.

Outside, he said to her:

—What d'you say that for?

Outside the close it was comparatively bright. Cannibal limped down along Dudhope Road, following Mags, not sure where, and not for the moment caring. Just glad to be breathing in cool, moist air. But the combination of exertion and the weakling warmth of the day made him realise he was burnt. His right arm was red, blistering up to the elbow, shirtsleeves charred, and his neck and left cheek pounded hot.

—Couldn't've pulled me out a spot earlier, could you?

She walked him onwards purposefully.

—We're going the wrong way, Cannibal suddenly realised.

—Plan was we'd meet up . . .

—Give us peace with plans, will you? Go back to Arran and Bubbles'll finish you off with a blowtorch.

—You got any other particular destination in mind?

—Hospital.

Cannibal stopped dead, ready to argue. But standing still made the boiling under his skin unbearable, so he walked on, sucking in great gulps of air, hoping he wouldn't faint in front of Mags. He didn't even complain when he got to the hospital and the doctor or nurse or whatever he was in a white coat, led him straight up to the Children's Wing, of all places.

They moved fast, these ghostly white figures floating around him. But whatever they were doing it felt good. Cold, freezing cold, and then bandaged up making him feel the way he used to feel when his mother tucked him up in bed when he wasn't well. Then they were saying something to him, beckoning him somewhere, these ghosts. He knew he was supposed to get up, but couldn't find the energy. They ended up pushing him up a long corridor that seemed to go on for ever, a bright, white light at the end of it, that got disappointingly greyer and a little greener as he approached the end. They put him in a bed and he lay there and watched Mags walk to the door. Probably he was just woozy and half asleep, but he thought he heard her talk some bollocks about missing him and loving him. That'd be why she left him in a burning kitchen, then. Just long enough to get him char-grilled, no more. She must have left while he was vomiting.

He woke up in the middle of the night, his blood like lava, melting away his insides. There was a nurse beside him, smiling at him.

—Not as bad as it seems, son, she said, and he believed her, went back to sleep again.

He woke up later. Morning, this time. A voice had woken him. A voice saying over and over again, 'Mummy, Mummy, Mummy', and he was scared stiff it was himself coming away with that. Jesus, please let it not be him. By the time he came round properly, he breathed a sigh of relief. The voice came from somewhere outside of the ward.

He looked around the room, the burns still nipping and slicing away at his arm and neck and cheek, but bearable now. He was surrounded by kids. All these wee bodies. He felt like a giant amongst them. The pain was bad, but not as bad as he'd feared. Nurse was right, the burns were sore but probably not that critical. He could move, anyway. He got up out of bed, and a nurse came up. He said he needed the bog and she helped him to the door, then left him. Inside, he checked his face in the mirror. Almost embarrassingly unburnt. A bit blistered, that's all. Like he'd fallen asleep on his side in the sun. His neck was bandaged up, but the little he could see underneath it looked satisfyingly worse. His arm was the sorest, but it was too well cotton-wooled and neatly packaged to see anything.

—How come I've landed in with the weans? he asked the nurse who brought him his breakfast.

Because he was one, she replied. He couldn't be annoyed with arguing. So he ate, turning his back on the yabbering and tottering playpen that looked like a deluxe doctors and nurses kit, bandages round heads and stookies and infusions on wheels that trundled along behind the miniature patients. They'd done a real job on one wee guy who was out cold on a bed, tubes poking out every which way and a machine by his side going bleep-bleep. Scary. The tubes and the smell gave Cannibal the shivers, and all that bleep-bleep-bleeping. The kid in the room beyond somewhere got his goat with his incessant Mum-mum-mummying. All night long he'd been going at it. And now, all morning too. What was wrong with the wee prick, for Chrissakes?

Cannibal checked his bedside cabinet – big yellow plastic bag in there with his gear in it. A nurse had said something about a doctor's round after breakfast. Give that a body-swerve. Somebody else came up when he'd finished his Frosties. Could've been another nurse, maybe you get plain-clothes nurses these days. Read his charts and looked very grave and businesslike the way they all do – teachers and social workers and the rest of them. Like there was always something dead serious going on and they had to try and make the likes of Cannibal realise that.

—The girl who brought you last night, said she was your sister?

Good for Mags.

—She also says you're sixteen.

—And I shouldn't be in here.

—She said she'd go directly home and bring your parents.

—Oh, you can depend on Margaret all right.

—Except no one's turned up yet. What school are you at?

—No, no. See, we're from out of town. Country types, my old dears, and we haven't got a phone so it'll take Margaret a wee while to bring them back from the cottage.

—Where is your parents' cottage?

—Glenochil. Miles away.

—What happened to you last night?

—Just as my sister said.

—I'd like to hear your version.

—Seriously, Nurse, if it's all the same to you, I don't think I'm up to it right now.

She looked him up and down but didn't ask any more questions. Told him there'd be a few people coming to see him, so he was just to stay put after the doctor's rounds. That'll be shining bright. There must be all hell let loose up at the Home. His absence would be noted by now, and they'd be on his trail. Time for some strategic planning.

He fiddled around with the plastic bag, keeping it inside his bedside cabinet, feeling around for the most basic clothes: jeans, T-shirt, trainers; leave the jersey. He transferred the jeans and T-shirt on to the plate that his hot breakfast was on, put the lid that served to keep it warm back over them. They were sticking out every which way, but if he moved fast enough, he might get away with it. He slipped his trainers on to his bare feet. The breakfast trolley was still outside the ward and Cannibal signalled to the nurse that he was just stepping outside to put his tray back. All smiles like a very cooperative and well-behaved boy.

The toilet in the corridor was being used, so he swore and looked around, wondered what to do next. He couldn't go back into his ward still holding the tray, so he took a chance on an unmarked door, and slipped inside. There was a boy standing, looking out the window. The room must've been about ten storeys up, because through the glass all there was was sky, and way, way below it, a little Polly Pocket city.

—Don't mind me.

He didn't wait for an answer but started at once to get into his jeans and T-shirt. He didn't look up at the boy, who didn't look at him either but just kept gawping out the window, which suited Cannibal fine. Then the boy said something that he didn't catch.

—What?

—Mummy.

—Fuck. You.

The boy still didn't look round. He was talking to the window. As if by bleating out over the city that lay before him he could trigger some deep maternal recognition and his old dear would look up from where she was walking, shopping or talking and though miles away and metres below him, she would see her son, realise his predicament, drop everything and come running.

—Shut it, Cannibal hissed, through clenched teeth and clamped jaws.

For the first time, the boy looked round at him, and it was a shock. Cannibal was looking at himself. The boy's head was as bald as Cannibal's, balder even, and he was as thin as him; two, three years younger, at the most. The boy said nothing, but just looked quietly and curiously at him, as if Cannibal might be worth pumping for some information about his mother.

—Stop greeting, will you? Driving everyone daft.

There was something beautiful about the boy, even Cannibal could see that, and it just made him madder. A beautiful version of himself. The bigness of his eyes, bigger than the sky behind him, and all that sadness for everyone to see. He shouldn't do that. Let everyone see. Gets everyone in a state.

—Mummy?

He said it directly to Cannibal, as if Cannibal maybe had the boy's ma stuck up his juke. Cannibal turned heels and ran for it. Out, down the corridor, the boy's chant following him along. Where was the kid's mother anyhow? Cannibal sloped through corridors and down staircases, hugging the walls so as not to attract attention, getting madder by the minute.

Then he was in a long corridor and had to make his way down it, peek through doors and in glass windows, on the lookout for a route that'd lead to the exit. Room after room was filled with people just lying there, dying, giving up the ghost. He wanted to go in, kick their beds, cause a disturbance. He'd rather see them writhing on the floor, screaming out, than just lying there, taking it, putting up with it. A few faces turned to look at him, old wrinkled faces, like something out of a nightmare, bald like him and the mummy's boy upstairs, their eyes dark, black, frightening, finished. Cannibal didn't care any more about not being seen, about being inconspicuous. He just wanted out. He ran wildly through the corridors, bouncing off the walls, throwing open doors until, at last, he found one that led out into the daylight, where he could breathe again.

He ran out the hospital gate and sat on a garden wall to catch his breath. When he looked up, Mags was there.

—Waited for you.

—Right.

And he wanted to drape himself around her warm, fat body out of gratitude, but knew he shouldn't. He nodded to her.

She said, —Cops've arrested Bubbles.

—What about the rest of you?

—We all agreed. Photie and Koff're saying they know nothing. Were in their rooms the whole time. I told the cops Bubbles tried to kill you. Built the bonfire, threw you in the room after he'd lit it.

—They buy it?

—Yeah. Trying to blow kids' eyes out with bangers? Setting the window sashes alight? Clearly a general mental case. I planked a few pieces of evidence in his room, too. They'll buy it.

Stoney's house was on the route between the hospital and the home, so they tried knocking on the door. No answer. There was nothing else for it but to go back to Arran House. Anyway, it'd help Mags and the others' story stand up if Cannibal returned wounded. Just, he'd have to get out of there smartly, a day or two at most, before the police or Janice or the social workers started on him in a big way. He wasn't up to that. He wouldn't be able to hold them off from calling his old dears either, and it was too early for that. The fire thing might still work out all right, letting Bubbles take the rap, but everyone assuming Cannibal was the key strategist. Soon enough Stoney's pay-off money'd come through and it was bound to be substantial, and cut four ways now instead of five. Then it'd be the time to go home, for a visit.

They arrived at Arran to something of a reception: Janice, the Director, the gang, a policeman, couple of carers, they were all there. Cannibal pleaded fatigue and pain, and got away with it because it was true. The tiredness and soreness got him through the next day too. He was visited by the home's GP who declared him fit enough not to be sent back to hospital, but ill enough not to be pressed too hard on the fire at number 17 Dudhope.

Sadly there had been no report in the papers. Not even the local ones, not even the freesheet. No one had been hurt, apart from him. No damage was done to any of the surrounding houses, precious little even to the basement itself. The fire brigade had arrived about ten minutes after Mags had whisked Cannibal off to hospital, and the fire had still been smouldering, producing a lot of smoke, but not enough to empty any of the flats in the tenement, including the lassie's upstairs.

Chances were that Bubbles would soon be back on the scene. For the moment they had moved him to an out-of-town locked Category A home, somewhere in Fife. He'd find his route one way or another, though, back to Cannibal.

Cannibal needed money. Stoney was staying incommunicado. Cannibal couldn't wait too long. Janice insisted that, although Cannibal's parents had been told something of the 'accident', they would have to be given the full details pretty soon, and he'd have to agree to see them. All he needed was the money for a train fare to London, a bit more for subsistence until he'd got a place to crash.

He stayed in his room for two whole days, letting them all file in – policeman, then policewoman, Janice every couple of hours, the Director twice a day, both days, the resident carer with her first-aid skills, the doc. Photofit and Koff called in every now and then and kept him up to date with what was going on. Mags kept herself scarce until the second night. Then she came armed with a can of cider, two pills, a mug of hot chocolate and her Parka zipped right up to the neck.

—This one's Mogadon, to be taken with the hot chocolate. The yellow one's a special wee present from me. Benzo, 25 mg Ativan. Chill pill for tomorrow. Before the long journey south.

Cannibal made space in the bed and flipped over the covers for Mags to come in.

—I'm too big. Don't fit.

All she could do was perch next to his pillow, her huge buttocks warming the side of his face that wasn't burnt.

—Time for me to venture beyond the sheltered security of The Minge, eh?

The Minge being Cannibal's pet name for Arran House. He'd once explained how he'd arrived at this sobriquet to

Mags and the gang: 'Arran, Arran sweater, yes? And therefore, sweat; a sweaty person is a smelly person. Minging, in other words. Ming sounds like minge, and seeing as how the place's full of fannies, hey presto, the perfect name.'

Mags nodded, and took hold of his hand.

—Yeah. Time's up.

—No dosh, though. Tell Stoney I'll want it pronto.

—Mug someone.

—OK.

Then she went, and Cannibal snuggled down in bed, enjoying the weakness of being ill the way he used to when he was wee. He was thinking Mags was all right for such a fat lump and was surprised to find himself becoming aroused. That ruined everything. Made him think of his old dear looking at him in that disgusted way of hers, and about Stoney, and about his wee sister finding his hoard of magazines.

Next morning he'd planned to be up with the lark, but slept in until past eleven, no one coming to wake him. He was feeling tip-top, his burns causing no more now than a prickly hot discomfort. He'd intended to make his getaway early doors. Now he'd have to wait. He got dressed, and sat in his room, walked up and down, played an old mouth organ his mother must've packed in with his gear ages ago. Janice and the others made their usual calls, and he told them all brightly that he'd soon be ready for school. Well, they said, let's see how it goes with your parents on Sunday.

Four o'clock was the optimum time to set off. Janice would be in her study, the boss in his office. According to Mags and the others, half the schools in the area were closed due to the weather – there'd been high winds all night, though Cannibal'd slept right through them – but most of the Arranites would be pretending to be going anyway, and most of the staff would be playing daft. So they'll be at the front door as usual, overseeing the clients straggling back in. Half three, Mags's pill popped, a pint of milk and a packet of Hobnobs pockled from the kitchen earlier downed, a bag of clothes and bits and bobs over his shoulder, another quiet wait for twenty minutes, and he was off.

Out the back door, over the wall, into the lane. Up round the patch of wasteland on to the far end of Dudhope where it doubled back on itself. For all the world like Dick Whittington, striding out on a cold and frosty morning, to seek his fortune. Make a man of himself. He turned out of Dudhope, and headed towards the top of Policy Road. Halfway there, two things happened. First, he began to feel giddy. He recognised the feeling but couldn't place it. The second thing was he saw a woman.

An old piss-pants, she reminded him of his gran, his old man's old dear. The woman's lips weren't moving as far as he could see but he'd bet his life that inside that old straggly head of hers she'd be going on and on about keeping your nose clean while keeping it to the grindstone and not sticking it up in the air. Old women like his gran expected a hell of a lot from noses. He looked down at his own nose and for a moment he thought it was melting from his face, which gave him a fright. Stop thinking about noses.

The woman's coat pissed him off. Her coat and her handbag. She wore the coat like his gran always did and his mum had started to, as though it was made of deflective material that could bounce people like Cannibal away from them. The woman gripped that shiny wee bag with its clip-snip clasp, like her life and all the lives of everyone she'd ever known were hidden away inside it.

Cannibal's giddiness got worse. The sandstone houses were collapsing around him, regressing back to just sand. Everything seemed to be collapsing, the tenements, lamp-posts, trees falling. Benzos don't do that, nor sulph nor doves, not even Hobnobs. It was his own imagination trying to stop him. Must be. Fact was he'd never tried his hand at a mugging before and it was turning out to be more of a challenge than he'd expected. Maybe it was some kind of divine intervention. Or maybe rotten luck – just be his Donald if the very time he chose for his first attempt at assault would be the exact moment of the destruction of the universe.

But if he concentrated hard, he found he could edit out the inconvenience of the death of the planet, long enough at least to get his hands on the old biddy's bag. Had to get money. He'd been in this situation before, concentrating beyond the immediate, but couldn't think when. Keep your mind on the objective. He had to get to London. No way he could go back to Arran House now, or worse, to his old estate. Too soon. Not enough achieved yet. Things had gone well enough so far, but Stoney still had to stump up and Cannibal needed to get that handbag. Only a few paces away from him now.

Up this close, he realised that he knew her, the old woman. Too late to change plans now, though he'd've preferred that she'd been a perfect stranger. Where had he seen her? At the home. The Guardian Angel. The staff and the Heidie always made a big thing about her. And she was nice enough. It was her daughter, the big fat one, that Cannibal couldn't stick. What was their name again? Something weird. Lapraik. Mrs Lapraik. Founder of Arran House. Shame it had to be her, but too late to change plans now. No point in worrying about it. Just 'cause he knew her didn't mean she'd know him. Wouldn't know him from Adam. Even to her. Arran House's Guardian fucken Angel, Cannibal wouldn't really exist. Not till this moment. She'd find out now, but.

F I V E

Just before he made his last approach towards his victim, Cannibal experienced something of a remission. His nose stopped bothering him and the houses around him had disintegrated totally. Houses, gardens, the street, the whole city lay in smoking debris all around. The worst of it over, Cannibal felt better. No need to shy away any more from exploding tenements at either side. If he was swaying, it was only because he had to step over tumbled lintels and fallen trees and splintered mahogany banisters. He knew none of these things was really there, that the place was perfectly intact around him, but if something appears to be in the way of progress, what can you do but negotiate your way round it?

He'd been here many times before. Could place it now. Not Ativan. Acid. Eejit, Mags. He knew that a part of your brain operates independently of the hallucinogen. That's the bit that you normally, when it's a good trip, cancel out. Times like these, you had to focus on it. Forget the visual trickery, ignore the palpitations and the cold sweat, keep cool, remember where you are, what you're about. In this case, all he had to do was get the bag, then he'd find some nice quiet place to let Mags's little present do its worst, pass over. It'd mean he'd have to be a bit more brusque than he'd intended. He had never snatched a bag before and didn't want it to seem personal against the old dear. Just get the bag and leave her in peace. But with his pulse racing and his eyes still playing tricks on him, if he was to be sure of success, he'd have to go at her uncompromisingly.

Bitch better have brownbacks on her, else his plan would be thwarted. Had to leg it to London before the day was out. Get deflected and, what with everything that's happened, he'd be picked up, sent back. Last chance saloon. He speeded up, tried editing out the wreckage all around him, see through the clouds of red dust and toppled carnage to the real, orderly, unchanged pavement that lay under his feet. He stopped for a second every now and then, took deep breaths, took control of himself. Only for a second, mind. Could feel the blood pumping though him, bowels beginning to churn, good sign that, stuff was moving through him, feel his skin, cold but supple, responding properly when he stretched his fingers out, bent his knee. At her again. Within a few feet of her now. A quick sprint and his fist would be round that bag. She, as much as he, wanted the whole thing over with.

But when he made the final grab, felt the bag in his hand, pushed the old dear over, he was convulsed with pain. He swore at himself; knew the pain wasn't real. Nothing wrong with him, just the acid. Another deep breath. Then he looked around, making sure the city hadn't started disintegrating again. It hadn't, but something else was happening. At first, for a split second, he thought he was rising up off the ground, but then realised he wasn't. It was the other way round, the earth was falling away beneath him. There was nothing pulling at him, nothing yanking him upwards, nothing around him at all. It was like he was standing still, but the street was being sucked down from under him. It was so sudden and so forceful that it seemed to have nothing to do with the tab. The street slurped, dragged itself away at an incredible rate, leaving Cannibal standing in mid-air, terrified, old Lapraik's bag in his hand. He tried desperately to push himself down towards the disappearing earth as it spiralled away from him, pawed at the air, screamed out.

The street that he'd stood on a split second earlier was now yards below him, perfectly reconstructed. He saw the pathetic old bint crumpled up in a heap on the pavement like a wino. She must've fallen funny, else he'd gone at her harder than he'd meant. The ground's pull away from him slowed after its first surge of acceleration. He felt that he wasn't so high yet that he couldn't clamber down. He let the bag drop, and watched it twirl down, down. If only he were next to something to cling on to, he could climb down, dreep off. But the trees and the tenements were out of reach, and the more he struggled to get at them, the faster they sank away from him.

Still kicking at nothing, Cannibal searched the scene below for something or someone to help him down, before it was too late. Dudhope Road, over the bowling green from South Policy, was a ribbon of white snow curling silently round below him, Arran House deserted, the gardens he'd once kept neat and trim perishing in the cold, gone to the dogs.

The only building higher than him now was the hospital, multistoreyed on top of a bare mound. It didn't seem so far away now as it did when you were on the ground. But it was still too far to reach. He tried running towards it, but with nothing to support him, no progressive movement was possible. A moment later, he could see behind the hospital and beyond it, past Dumbarton Road, over the river and the houses beyond the river. The whole country was plunging away from him. He could feel his heart pounding, the panic rising. He repeated over and over to himself that it wasn't possible, that it was an hallucination, it would pass. The city opened up below him, under his dangling feet. Its towers and turrets and high-rises paltry and mean from up here, caked in soiled sleet. Half dead, almost immobile, the few people scattered around refusing to look up, like Mags's silenced jinns, bearing their privacy like a habit they couldn't shake. There was no use in shouting out, for nothing could be heard. Except his own heartbeat, ramming at his ribcage. Still he cried and called out for his ma, between swearing and yelps of terror. Stuck up there, flailing around against nothing, nothing at all, not even air or wind, not even the sky taking any notice of him.

As the whole city drained away below him, he gave in fighting against the nothingness and sobbed. So lonely. No one else, no *thing* else, just him and that skinny body of his that held him up there. Below, nothing between him and his sad, deflating city, silence built into its very foundations. Around it, the tear of the river, and the rocks and sediment pierced with small, red holes that bled sandstone, crusting into tenements. Further out, shorn hills, naked and frosted, the sea shivering around ancient crags trying to push themselves back down under the world's surface.

Floating adrift like that, his body turned and twisted of its own accord. Best he could do was throw his bodyweight all in the one direction and wait for the air current to swing him around. When it did, he found himself facing north-wards towards his old estate. The sight of it woke him from the faint that was engulfing him; its grey concrete lay still and white and shapeless, like mist that had seeped down from the tiny hills behind. It surprised him how close the place was to the rest of the city. His head spun, his heart thundered, bolting painfully through his veins. He kept his eyes on the distant, minuscule streets of his childhood, saw people converge on the them, heard the tinkle of the ice-cream van, dogs barking. The only sign of life for miles and fathoms around and he couldn't move towards it.

On the point of passing out, he felt the city below him beginning to rise slowly again. He tried to take a mental picture of the streets that led to his part of town, but they were so convoluted, severed by parking lots and office blocks and one-way systems; too complex to commit to memory. But the warmer currents created by the city's return from the chasm carried him northwards anyway, towards his estate. Then, just before everything went dark, he cried 'Ma' once more, and thought he heard her voice call out his name.

3

S I X

—Fuck women. At least, that's what it looked like.

—Christ.

Colin shuffled in his seat, glanced at the ward clock.

It was true. Yesterday, as she lay in bed, staring up at the ceiling as usual, her eye caught a glimpse of someone peering in at the ward door. She turned and, the way the light was, she could hardly see him. Just enough to know it was a him and that he was mouthing something. It looked like 'fuck women'. Maybe it wasn't, but it'd be a good story to tell Colin. Make him squirm.

—What do you think he meant, Col?

—Pretty obvious, isn't it?

—Not necessarily. He could have meant several things. Maybe he meant that he would like to. Fuck women. Of course it might just have meant, Fuck off, Women. All women. Then again, maybe it was advice. Fuck, woman.

Maybe he thought I should take it up. Perhaps it'd been his miracle cure and he was suggesting I give it a go.

—For God's sake.

—Maybe I *should* give it a go, this fucking. What d'you reckon?

—How should I know?

Colin checked the clock again, which pissed her off.

—Have you done it, Col?

—That's private.

—You used to tell me everything.

—That was before.

—Before what?

She should let him go, but couldn't.

—When I get out, d'you think I should?

—Should what?

—Fuck Simon.

—Give us a break, Paris, will you?

As usual, Colin had come late, left early. All Paris could do after that was wait for the next meal, the next visit. Her dad probably. Then again, maybe not. This wasn't an ordinary week. This was the week she was getting out. This Thursday coming, she'd be home, back to life again. So maybe she wouldn't get all the usual visits, what with Mum tidying up the house and Dad repainting her room.

She lay back, tried to relax, conserve her energy. Problem was, she had to keep her eyes open all the time she lay in the hospital bed. Even a blink could trigger a terrifying burst of moon.

Her mother had explained that moon to her a long time ago. Why it was behind bars, why it looked so angry. For years after, it never bothered her. Then, when she got sick, that big fat moon presented itself to her again every time she closed her eyes. Glaring at her, getting closer, straining behind its prison bars.

So she had to lie there staring purposefully up at the ceiling. Luckily a lifeless, pasty, job-lot hospital-green ceiling, easy enough to dissolve away and let some other image take its place. She could do that thing they say you can do with coal fires – see pictures in the flames. She could stare at the cracks that laddered the ceiling from corner to corner; make pictures out of the scaly patches; force the cheap plaster that flaked from the scurf to take on some other shape.

A leaf. She knew that leaf. That particular leaf. From the tree in the garden outside number 8, across the street and down a bit from her beloved number 17 Dudhope Road. A tree of every imaginable red. The trunk one red, the underside of the leaf another, the topside another. Every year the three parts of that tree went through every shade of red you'd ever heard of. In winter, reddy browns. Then browny reds: ripe sloes, copper, bronze. In summer, the top-leaf crimson, the underside like scarlet underwear, the trunk suntanned like a mature Mediterranean lady. Fading to pretty, yellowy reds in autumn. An astonishing tree. Sometimes it shed its leaves on the pavement, and in the morning they lay there splattered around, like evidence of a murder the night before. You never knew when its leaves would fall; it just happened, unannounced, at odd times of the year.

The whole street was like that. Disorganised. There was an apple blossom, a little runt of a tree that someone sometime had cut away at. None of its branches had grown out again, but the tree kept on flowering, its stunted little twigs discharging deformed leaves, and always at the wrong time. At Christmas, when all the other trees that towered around it looked hangdog and emaciated, that midget tree blossomed with an impish flourish, sticking a thousand rude little tongues out at nature.

—And how are we today?

Nurse Simms. Just arrived on backshift. No time for slouching now, time for Paris to brush up her act.

—I'm good, Morag. Thanks.

And she tried to look good. Healthy, jaunty.

—That's the spirit. Got to live up to that fancy name of yours, eh? Can't have Paris looking like a wet day in Govan, now can we?

Paris tried to smile. Not too much. Just stretch the corners of the mouth a little, and don't hold it for too long. Got to play it carefully with Morag, this week of all weeks.

Paris's name really pissed Morag off. To be fair, it pissed off a hell of a lot of folk. It might be all right being called Paris in Surrey or Sevenoaks, or New York, or in Paris even, but not in a big industrial city like this. Just got people's backs up. Of course, her mum and dad thought it was a great idea. Still do. Have done, ever since their honeymoon.

What happened was, her mum and dad had sworn to each other that as soon as they were married they would somehow get themselves to Paris. Course, it never happened. Mum found she was pregnant a month before the wedding, then Dad put the tin lid on it by getting himself laid off. So they had themselves a weekend down the Clyde Coast – a wet and windy honeymoon weekend that lasted them for the whole of their lives. They spoke about it that often – how they walked along the beach, got on the kiddies' merry-go-round, got chased by the man, ran away laughing – that Paris felt she'd been with them. Well, she had. She could remember them, perfectly remember peeping out Mum's belly button and seeing Dad, his hair not yet grey, trousers rolled up; her mum's skirts howked up into her tights. The two of them paddling, the sea lapping lazuli over their ankles, so cold it turned their feet blue too. Saw Dad kicking the water up, and the salty drops falling, frothing slowly, over Mum, who squealed like a girl, which was all she was back then.

They reckoned that Troon was every bit as good as France could ever have been and decided on the Sunday morning, lying in bed in the B & B, that they would call the baby, who was starting to unpick for ever and a day the musculature of its mother's abdomen, Paris, in honour of that blissful weekend. Could hardly've called her Troon.

Morag would no doubt have been happier with Troon. Throughout all the months Paris had been under her care she hadn't managed to utter her name without tacking on a little joke of her own. Always with a smile, of course. One of those big, sunny smiles of hers that got your goat. And you had to smile back; show you weren't uppity about such things. Not too broadly, mind, in case she thought you were laughing at her. Too much of a smile would be a mistake. This week was crucial. What Morag would say in the little glass office to the senior nurses, comments she might pass to some doctor or other in the corridor, it all must count for something. Maybe Morag even made an official report; you never knew. Those casual conversations at the end of the bed, Morag holding court with sundry other medicals and with Paris's family – her mum trying too hard to look concerned, Dad trying too hard to look unconcerned, Colin looking just angry as usual – all of that had more to do with next Thursday going ahead, she was sure, than all the graphs and charts and blood counts and ultrasounds and CAT-scans.

—What d'you say I pop round later and give you a makeover?

As if they'd happened to meet by chance in a café in the west end. Later they'd fool around with lipstick and blush. Girls, eh.

—Can't have you going out into the big, bad world looking less than dazzling.

—Certainly not, Morag.

Morag, Paris reckoned, still lived at home. With a mother no doubt, who thought she was an absolute treasure, but secretly also a bit of a disappointment. Paris had her very own infallible way of checking birth dates, without even having to ask, so she knew Morag was forty. But for anyone else, it'd be hard to tell – Morag being that rounded and mumsy, hair in a £20 demi-wave, naff clothes – she could be anywhere from her mid-thirties to nigh on fifty. She must've been the kind of stout, awkward girl whom the others laughed at and that Paris, the old Paris, had always made it her duty to defend. Poor Morag – if you weren't fanciable, or ran with the wild girls, or not one of the clever ones, the only option left was to be nice. If you got to be forty or so and still didn't have a life, what else could you do but pretend to care? Care about other folks' lives. And here was Paris now – the victim of Morag Simms' caring. Paris wished she'd ripped the pish out of her pudgy type all along.

—Right. That's you booked in for the full beauty treatment and manicure, madam. Practice run for lover boy, eh? Be back once I've done me rounds, Morag said gaily, and tucked the single sheet that was already tucked tightly round Paris tighter, and said she'd catch up with her later, waddled off.

Look straight up at the old fitment where the central light for the whole ward used to hang but was now just a hole in the chapped rash of the ceiling, and imagine it was the big bay window in the front room in Dudhope Road. Look past the apple blossom, narky and bare in spring when it should've been flowering, across the street into other people's lives. At the woman directly opposite whom

Paris had never spoken to, never even seen in the street, but thought was so elegant in all her Versace and Benetton and her bust-up old open-top MG and her new baby at thirty-odd. At the two men – in the next close to the woman – who live together and always smiled over at her, and seemed so strong and settled. Paris had never seen them fight – but she saw the woman, terrific and savage like a leopard, splicing up the poor father of her child who only got to stay over every now and then. In the flat above, the family from Montserrat fought too, sometimes at the same time as the woman below, without either party knowing. Their fights were a different sort of affair altogether, flinging themselves joyously into entire-family rages.

Look down the road to see tenements like Paris's on one side, big detached houses on the other, the first one a children's home of some sort. Wild, bedraggled kids that ran riot and sometimes fought viciously and other times played gently with the well-turned-out toddlers from the house next door. A group of them had taken over the basement flat below her house a while ago, and made a right nuisance of themselves, setting the place on fire and whatnot. Further down and there was a house that everyone liked to say used to be a brothel. At the very end of the street, the playpark. The street ended there. Behind it, high on an embankment, ran the railway line, and overlooking that, the hospital where Paris lay now. Her room was on the other side of the hospital building, so she couldn't see her street, but in her mind she pictured it as a kind of tunnel. Bushy with shops and people at the top, canopied with trees down to its depth at the park. Her beautiful road a conveyor belt, funnelling her life down past the swings and seesaws of her childhood, past houses and hedges and trees all the way down and beyond, to this sullen, grey hospital of hers.

She was getting tired, her dry eyes smarting at the broken skin of the ceiling, no longer able to conjure up the view from the window of the front room of her home. Anyway, it was time to get ready for the makeover, attract Morag's attention, show herself willing. Morag offered every day to tidy her up but since Paris had told Simon to stay away, she couldn't see the point.

—Don't come back, Si, she'd told him.

—I don't want you to see me here, like this, any more. When I get home, *then* you can come and see me. Deal?

Si had nodded gravely, sadly, but Paris couldn't get the notion out of her head that the moment he was out of the hospital grounds he'd have punched the air and yelped: Yes!

It was a dangerous tactic, turning down Morag's offers. The makeover was one of Morag's little gifts to her charges. Spurn them, and you risked losing her patronage. This week, Paris had to be sure that Morag, like God, was on her side. Morag could trash the whole getting-out deal, no problem. Anyhow, Dad might yet pass by after tea this evening and with her face on, and wig, nail-varnished, Paris'd be better equipped to lash out at him. Unslumped and sitting up nice in bed, she looked around for Morag, who was attending to someone in the third bed up on the opposite side, the bed Lorraine had occupied until last month. Paris made a face which was supposed to convey the complicated message 'I'm ready when you are', and it must have worked, 'cause Nurse Simms made her way slowly over.

—I'm ready and set to be dolled up by expert hands. If you've a moment now, I mean.

—That a girl. Always got a moment for my Paris. Let's go the whole hog, eh?

She took a little bag of makeup from the bedside cabinet, and sat down.

—Remembered a social engagement today, have we?

—Just Dad.

—Well, we girls don't fix ourselves up for other people, do we? We do it for ourselves. Matter of self-esteem, isn't it?

Rich coming from Morag. Whose civvies announced to the world the pointlessness of properly dressing such a dumpy unwanted anatomy. While Morag unzipped, uncorked and screwed the caps off the various phials and caskets, Paris looked down, past Morag's hands poised like a painter's before a blank canvas, at her own body: her arms and legs not as stringy as they had been, her colour not quite as drained. She used to think her body was, not exactly beautiful, but cheerful at least. Happy breasts, her eager tummy pushing its way just slightly out towards the world, and below, the unusual concave line of her pubic hair, like a smile. She had shown her body to Simon a few times, and it was like sharing a secret, a delightful joke. It still hadn't recovered that good humour yet, still stared back, annoyed, but wasn't quite as narked as it had been. Her thighs still looked flaccid, belying the tight grip they clamped her sex in, keeping it shut off and airless, closing down any contact between her sinister internal machinations, and the outside world. She couldn't even shit, for Chrissakes, though according to the Walking Ironing Boards, as Lorraine and she used to call the various medics with their starched, touch-me-not overalls, that was more down to the cocktail of chlorambucil and cyclophosphamide, which they also told her caused her occasional avalanche of prodigious diarrhoea. Should have a fancy name, a cocktail as spectacular as that. *Mount Etna (Only Erupts Once in a Thousand Years. But Boy ...). Dappled Beauty.*

Don't think about horrible stuff like that. Think about Simon again. She'd taken off her clothes for Si, first time, after a friend of theirs had bent over a chair and asked them, along with three or four others in the room, to look up inside her. She was seventeen this girl, they all were, and drunk, and they hardly knew her: a friend of a friend whose parents' house they'd ended up in after the pub. The girl was convinced she had some kind of blockage. Everyone laughed and told her she was talking nonsense, so she took off her pants, pulled up her skirt, bent over, pulled her buttocks apart and asked them all to see for themselves. Of course no one came near her, but howled, in a mix of disgust and hilarity, at the girl's audacity.

Rather than excited by it, Simon'd been made anxious by the display. The next night Paris undressed in the bathroom of her house and, with her parents out, walked in naked to the big room where Simon was waiting. He was shocked but pleased, didn't insist on them taking it further, and the two of them laughed, happy and relaxed. In the two years since, they had repeated the performance maybe five or six times, twice when he too took off his clothes. Once she took his hand and let it graze the down on her back and hips and thighs, and Simon would have taken it further then. So would Paris, but took fright when she saw in her mind's eye, her moon. In the guise of a hooker's thigh. A prossy her and Si'd seen in a grotty bar they'd gone into once to ask directions. She just sat there, hugely. Her white, bare thigh and the colossal curve of her buttock behind the legs of the table, exactly like the bars around Paris's moon.

Paris thought of the drunk, exhibitionist unknown girl now, as she lay in front of Morag with her nightdress riding up around her legs. She despised the girl at the time, thought she was making a play for the boys, eclipsing the more modest sexuality of Paris and the other girls. But

now, knowing what it was to be dependent on the progno-
sis and judgements of others, having unctuous doctors and
mawkish nurses take charge of your blockages and
leakages, cracked skin and inflamed cavities, get involved in
the pain of passing water and stools, she felt differently
about the episode. Summoning up the scene in her mind,
she saw the girl's face as if for the first time: peering round
behind her own naked rump, imploring, fretful, at her
exhilarated inspectors. The horror of needing others to tell
you about your own body. The thing you should know most
about, but knew less than everyone else around you. The
girl was drunk and scared and locked inside her own flesh,
hoped that someone on the outside could sort her out.

—You're beginning to look presentable already.

Morag. Paris's mind had a habit of forgetting there were
people around her, even if they were painting her or sticking pins in her, or inspecting or washing parts of her she
wished they wouldn't. Morag liked to talk when she was
painting up her clients.

—In no time we'll have you looking like someone who
deserves to be called Paris.

—Steady on.

—Must admit. It's a hard one to live up to. A Paris
really *has* to be beautiful, doesn't she?

Morag chattered on as usual while she added the final
touches to her masterpiece. A dash of eye pencil where
there was precious little brow; a stipple of liner on bare,
raw skin; a puff of powder on pale cheeks. Paris didn't
listen. She had perfected the art of the interested glance,
the appreciative Hmm, cocking her head to one side every
now and then, subliminally taking in the odd word so she
had some idea of the theme in case of questions. She'd
learnt the trick on her one visit to France – not Paris, but
Brittany – a school trip, where her name demanded she

feign a better knowledge of French than the rest of the group. She'd perfected the act in clubs where she could never hear a word for the music, but pretended she could. She used to be thought a good listener, the old Paris. Interested in everyone.

At first, she didn't mind Morag's little parables. At least they broke the monotony; sermons designed to make her patients realise there were others worse off than themselves; fables which illustrated correct frames of mind. All of them springing from within the hospital itself – Morag's entire world. Stories from other countries down the corridor: exotic wards on Level Three, the culinary shortcomings of the West Wing, foreign lifestyles in the East. Who was getting out, who never would, which patients fancied which nurses, which sister was having an affair with a married porter. But despite the bigness of the hospital world, teeming with its multitude of unknown victims and long-suffering professionals, Morag's stories soon took on a repetitive nature. The morals that lay behind them, banal. Luckily, on this occasion there were no questions, no expectation of a reply. Morag clipped and clicked and twirled, shut her bag of potions and prepared to continue her good work elsewhere.

—The way you look, I'd let you out today.

—If only you were the boss, Morag. You know more than all the rest of them put together with all their degrees and diplomas.

It worked. Morag gave her an unconvincing unconvinced look, smiled, and set off with a spring in her step. And Paris sat there, bolt upright, feeling the creams and powders on her face like a child forced to have her face painted up like a cat's or a clown's because its parents were determined it enjoy itself. The heavy wig holding her head together, nails varnished but with nothing to do with them she sat there dumb and feeling stupid. Sat there for ages, disturbed only by the auxiliary who brought her her tea, and then the woman on her right, slumped in the chair by her bed staring at her telly, who asked,

—Time's it, dear?

—Twelve. Ish.

—Day or night?

—Day.

You'd think the telly programmes would provide a clue. But the old dear never saw it, just stared at it. All her attention was on her insides; on her private battle. Sometimes, some of the happy-clappy lot'd appear in the ward – ministers or nuns or support-group workers, various new-fangled therapists – and they'd try and conjure up that old wartime spirit, as if the women in here were all hiding out in an Anderson shelter, waiting for the raid to be over with. What they never realised was that they weren't in it together, this army of wounded women. There was no common enemy. Each of them just fighting their own private wars, preferably with as little interference from outside as possible. Dying alone.

Except that Paris wasn't dying any more. That was a fact. Not just because it was official – everyone said so. Mum, Dad, Col, Simon on the phone – but because Paris herself had decided. For the first two years after her diagnosis she assumed she was going to die. Sat for day after day at her big bay window looking out, glumly, taking off to her bed for the odd few days when things got rough. When they brought her into hospital she absolutely knew that was The End. Game a bogey. Then, couple of weeks back, her name disappeared off The List.

A simple list of names that appeared in her head, quite clearly marked with dates of births and deaths. Paris's own name used to be on it, right there at the very top, and now, suddenly, it wasn't. Just disappeared after her last cycle of radiotherapy. Not long after, they told her that she was getting out. Everything had improved since then. She tried telling her mum and dad and Colin and Si about The List and how her name had been taken off it and they all smiled patiently. So what. *She* could see The List, and since her name had been dropped from it, even that leering, shrieking moon glowered over her a little less.

Paris decided to check The List again, make sure there'd been no changes since the last bulletin. She kept her eyes open and directed them to the ceiling above the nurses' glass office where the signal for The List was most easily and clearly picked up. She concentrated hard and finally a picture, crackly at first, settled down and a computer-type screen appeared in front of her eyes: The List, complete with flashing cursor which she could move around at will.

Frances McFarlane (née Bradford)	1951–2008
Brian Craig McFarlane	1950–2036
Colin 'Troon' McFarlane	1978–2036
Lorraine Broadie	1971–1997
Simon Crichton	1977–2057
Morag Simms	1957–2011

And the list went on, names of half-forgotten schoolfriends and teachers, distant cousins, fellow students, you name it. Names that didn't ring a bell at all. Unfortunately, it wasn't in any alphabetical or chronological order (if she herself, or some wacky insightful part of her, was the author, then that figured: Paris had never been the most methodical of people), and she'd never managed to scroll her way to the end. Maybe, if she kept on scrolling for ever, the list would be universal, start flashing up names like Ghita Hussein and Rafael Leandro Hernandez and Siao-Lai Noh or whatever.

What it wouldn't give, The List, was more classified details. Days and months; causes of death, etc. But there was enough information there to check against verifiable facts. Nurse Morag *was* born in 1957. Paris'd asked her and when Morag wouldn't volunteer the year, Paris did. Morag wanted to know how she knew, but naturally Paris couldn't give her source. The List was highly confidential information. For Her Eyes Only. You couldn't go around telling folk willy-nilly when they were going to die.

The List gave Paris food for thought. For instance, Brian McFarlane outliving Frances McFarlane by nearly thirty years? Paris would've sworn blind it'd've been the other way around: that her mum would have driven Dad to an early grave. Still, it was fair enough; Dad rather liked life. Mum found it all a bloody nuisance. And what about Colin going out the same year as Dad? Car accident involving the two of them, perhaps? Poor old Morag was only going to last to her fifties – she'd get overweight and stressed, have an early stroke, no doubt about it.

Worst of all was Lorraine – she was that triumphant on getting out of here before Paris and trying not to show it, but the Big C's still hot on her tail. Old Si's up there in the high numbers, eighty before he'd push off. Who knows, maybe Paris will be burying him? (That is, if she didn't chuck him long before that, give back the engagement ring and have a wild time of it the next few years. Make up for lost time.) Was it possible that she herself could live that long? Who could tell, now that her name had been taken off The List? It used to read:

Paris Frances McFarlane   1976–1997

but with the 1997 flashing, as though the final date had yet To Be Confirmed. Then, fortnight or so ago, once she'd got over the godawful tiredness of her last radiotherapy session and the skin on her eyelids had stopped burning, it disappeared. She'd tried scrolling through as much as she could, to see if her name turned up somewhere further down The List, but had never found it. It'd always been right at the top, followed by the names of the people she knew best. No reason why it should've been moved.

She wasn't going to die. Simple as that. It all fitted: her sickness was only rarely fatal in women of her age. And though her GP and the hospital clinic had lost time farting around with theories and losing her notes, and wondering if this feeling that her blood was on fire, the constant colds, the depression, wasn't all in her mind. (Girls, eh.) But in the end, they must've caught it in time. Everything was just taking longer than expected. Being in hospital's like waiting for a delayed train or plane. Everyone keeps saying she'd be getting out, getting out, and then they'd decide to give her one more dose of this or one of that, keep her in a tad longer. Never any announcement over the loudspeakers giving definite schedules.

This time, though, for sure. The Head Honcho doctor said it. Dressed it up in all sorts of medicspeak, of course, with a few ifs and buts thrown in. Probably obligatory these days, for insurance purposes. And anyway, Paris *knew*. She'd felt a warmth – as opposed to a burning – somewhere deep inside her. Faint, but definitely there, for a whole week now.

Thursday: 17 Dudhope Road. Mum and Dad and Colin and pots of tea. Simon calling round. Maybe a kiss – if he could summon up the courage. Her big room. Her street. Her tree.

—It was a girl called Charlotte planted that red tree. Last century. She lived in the kids' home, before it was a home.

—How d'you know that?

Paris passed some of the time she'd spent in hospital thinking up stories to tell to Morag, pass them off as true.

—Local history book. Just picture it, Morag. No tenements yet, just the odd villa and farmhouse. Nothing up the road there but green, rolling hills. Blue skies. Ball of yellow sun, the whole scene like a child's painting. Birds chirping happily away. And there's our Charlotte, in the big, green garden, down on her hunkers, scrabbling around in the earth.

—Planting her tree?

—Hands going pit-a-slap-plump as she pats down the earth around the tiny tree. Not red yet, more baby pink. Then up she gets, Charlotte, and scampers back to the big house. Inside – the contrast! – gloomy gloomy gloomy. All dark polished mahogany and gaslights. Smell of linseed and polish. Shivering floorboards and draughty window-frames. Big, gruff grandfather clock, too dignified to *tick*, just *tock-tock-tocks* away sternly in the hall. In the kitchen, Jenny's baking.

—Who's Jenny?

—Jenny Goudie. In service with Charlotte's family. There she is, in a blur of flour. Around her, a feast of Abernethy biscuits and Ballater scones.

—You're making this up.

Jenny sits the little girl up on the butcher's block and carries on working, baking, chopping, while Lonely Little Charlotte complains about having no friends to play with. Then Jenny goes out and helps the little girl to build a little protective cylinder round the sapling tree.

—Must've worked, 'cause you ought to see that tree now.

Over the months, Paris had developed the Charlotte story, and others, for Morag. She filled in the Victorian scene: the rail track still there, where it is now, but with steam trains chugging picturesquely along; the first few tenements appearing; her tree growing under Charlotte's tender care. She had Charlotte live an uneventful life as the city grew up around her.

—Stayed a spinster all her days. Eventually became ill and housebound, shouting at passing kids to keep their manky hands off her tree.

Morag didn't like the ending, but Paris thought that Morag of all people ought to have known what living in this city does to you. Marinades us all in grime, cold-smokes you in fog and spite, till hearts are bitter-pickled, souls leathered.

This week she'd have to be on her best behaviour, especially with Morag. Make sure there were no stumbling blocks in the plans to let her home. She missed winding Morag up, dreaming up silly tales for her, swearing blind they were true.

The red tree's next owner, she decided, was a Mr Ernest Findlayson, who lived at number 6 between the wars. She made him Professor of Engineering at the university. A small and elegantly dressed chap, polite to his neighbours. Ernest took special care of the tree Charlotte had planted half a century earlier. Pruned it, watered it, checked it daily for any signs of disease. And he wrote about it. When the next owners took over the house after his death they found endless diaries packed full of descriptions of that red little ornamental plum tree.

Over the years Ernest referred to the tree by different names. Sometimes they were affectionate: Petal, Nutbrown, Berry, Princess, Woody. Other times they were more in keeping with Ernest's scientific calling: Blossom, Sylvia, Arboria. For four or five notebooks in a row he used cold, scientific names, as if he and the object of his love were going through a sticky patch and had resorted to formalities: Rosacea, Corolla, Prunus.

Towards the end of his life, right after the formal period, he began to use more womanly names. Camilla, Cleopatra, Sappho, Beatrice, Carmen. (He would have given the tree a Scottish name, but Paris couldn't think of any sensual Scottish goddesses.) His notes concerning the tree, originally botanical and scientific in nature, began to read like love letters. He serenaded the opulence of her bark (later, skin); waxed lyrical about how her branches stretched out and opened, like arms (later, legs) welcoming him in. In daylight, sifting the breeze through her leaves, she cooled him; at night, warmed him with her ruby glow.

Then, Paris had him not turning up for his lectures at the university, kept back by the tree's womanly attentions. She – Paris – had him spotted in his garden at all sorts of times, night and day, tending or talking to or touching his beautiful tree. Ernest wanted to unite himself with his tree. His books became filled with frantic notions of how he could graft himself and the tree together, speculations on the possibility of germinating the seed of her fruit, adhering his own seed to cross-fertilise the two of them, achieve a hybrid of them both. Beautiful, detailed drawings of fronds, stigmas, carpels, gynoecia, ovules and stamens filled page after page.

—It's a psychiatrist you need, Paris McFarlane, not a nurse. I blame your mother. That's what you get when you give your children ridiculous names.

Precisely how he went about applying his theories, Paris left to Morag's imagination.

—No one knows what happened exactly, in the end. Just that Ernest Findlayson suddenly disappeared from sight, leaving no trace, his house in a mess, with notes and drawings scattered everywhere.

—That's a very nasty little story, Paris. You disappoint me.

—And I lied to you about Charlotte, Morag. In fact she died in childhood. I didn't want to upset you. And her parents buried her beside the tree she'd planted. I reckon Ernest must've known that, and it was one of the things that made the tree so fascinating for him. So you see, Morag, now tree, child and man are united for ever in perennial fecundity.

Morag complained to Paris's mother about the story which she thought was tasteless and a worrying indicator of Paris's state of mind.

Which showed how dangerous a game it was. For all Paris knew, Morag could've reported her to the hospital authorities too. So, this week, she refrained from telling any more stories. Just lay in her bed and dreamt them up silently to herself.

By evening visiting time, she was tired. Mum and Dad arrived, and Dad produced with a TA-TA-RA-RA! a bundle of brochures for Weekend Breaks in Paree. (In the McFarlane family they always refer to Paris, France as *Paree* to avoid confusion with Paris, McFarlane.) Their celebration for her recovery. Just as soon as she was well enough, they'd all go off to the city of her birthright. First time any of them had been there. Dad said he'd book it for the end of April next year. That'd be time enough, eh?

Mum, trying to be businesslike, quizzed Morag about blood counts and bone marrow suppression and other such matters about which of course she didn't have a scooby. Dad trying to think up epigrammatic little nuggets and not coming up with any. Plenty of time to talk next week. She couldn't wait. Couldn't wait to be with her family again. Once she was home she'd stop tormenting them. Give over needling Colin, ignoring Dad, criticising Mum. She'd be normal. A nice twenty-one-year-old, about to go back to college with any luck. Just that, right now, tonight, she wished they'd piss off out of here. Which they did.

Night night. Kiss kiss. Room's almost ready for you. Take care.

And then Dad, whispering: —Moon?

—Sod it.

—You tell it.

Then sleep. Moon did appear. Rattled its cage, but only briefly. Backed off at Paris's growl. Sleepsleepsleep.

In the morning her dad was standing in front of her, smiling, looking more relaxed than he had since this whole business started. Paris was confused. This wasn't the day she was being allowed out. There were three – no two now was it? – days to go. Dad leant forward and lightly took her hand. His hair had grown and brushed her cheek and neck.

—You need a haircut. Want me to do it for you?

Once, when she was little, she set about his head with scissors when he was asleep. Not the plastic ones out of her doctor's kit which she often used to pretend to cut his hair with, but real ones. Dad'd smiled, slumbering, until the sharp metal snip-crunch woke him with a jump. It had been a joke ever since, that one day she'd cut his hair again.

—No thank you. I'm not that badly paid.

Wasn't her dad. It was Nurse Geraldine, looking down at her, puzzled. One of the nice nurses, Geraldine. Just as well. If it'd been Morag, that moment of waking confusion would've been a black mark on Paris's record. Something not quite right. Something to let doctors know about. Nurse Geraldine just smiled and said a few morning pleasantries, then left Paris with her tea and a plate of multi-coloured pills, enough to fill a beanbag with.

Tired this morning. Scalp itchy. Thank God Morag wasn't on duty. Could keep her hair off. Close the eyes. Moon? Nope. Excellent, excellent.

Thank *God* Morag's not on duty? Blasphemy. Keep God – god? – out of this. This Evil's an abomination in his – His? – eyes. Mum and Dad should've sent her to church or Sunday school or something. Least she'd know how the capital letters worked. D'you use them only if you believe in Him – him? No problem with the capital E for Evil, but. That exists all right. Been slithering its revolting way through her body for over two years now. Don't think about it. It likes you to think about it. You can feel it growing inside you when you think about it. Likes to get you on your own, Evil. Like when it's got you in one of those big machines, all to itself. Stuck inside a big, too-clean tube, burning your skin. Don't think about it. That's what It wants, Evil.

Think about Evil and Good later, when it's all over. Thursday.

Lunchtime, Nurse Geraldine joined Paris for a chat. Paris hadn't had much practice in normal chit-chat of late. Some of her friends passed by from time to time, and either they sat terrified, as if she might at any moment pounce on them, poison them with her bat's blood, or they'd talk twenty-to-the-dozen about pop groups and film stars whom Paris found hard to believe still existed.

She'd try to talk to them about what was going on with her, but they always wanted to change the subject. They weren't interested in discovering that cytotoxic drugs operate by destroying the entire cell. Particularly fast-dividing cells, like those in the gut lining, fingernails and hair. Reason why she was bald.

Her poor hair.

—Spun gold, her dad used to always say.

—Spun gold. From all the honey smiles that were poured on you when you were a kid.

He was right too. She could remember prancing around in front of various aunties and neighbours and being the apple of everyone's eye. Lapping up their claps and pats and admiring looks and compliments. And now, nobody understands why Paris, sick Paris, insists on a black wig. Doesn't go with your colouring they tell her. You'd look much better in a blonde one. We can get you one that's the same shade as your own hair. No one'll know the difference. Thing was, her new hair was beginning to grow back in wiry, patchy clumps. But much darker.

She told Geraldine, over tea, all about her spun gold hair and the honey smiles. Then Geraldine told her a story. This was not normal for Geraldine. It was a story that Morag had told her but, amazingly, had not yet told Paris. Nurse Geraldine said Morag called the story:

ONE MAN'S SEARCH FOR BEAUTY

and it began:

There was once a man who considered himself to be quite the ugliest man on the planet. Not that he had any deformity or particular affliction – that would at least have given him an excuse for his unattractiveness. No, he was simply small, with irregular features, a small nose maybe, or eyes too wide apart, or sticky-out ears. Morag hadn't filled Geraldine in on the precise details. She'd merely said that he was particularly unattractive.

It was his great grief in life. There are plenty of unattractive people in the world. Morag had told Geraldine, but they don't dwell on it, they accept it and find a way to deal with it.

—She means herself, of course. Morag.

Geraldine laughed and said,

—I couldn't possibly comment.

—Morag likes to let you know that she's one for taking the good with the bad and getting on with life.

—Nothing wrong in that, I suppose.

—Course not. Carry on, Geraldine.

Unlike Morag, this man could never accept his burden in life. Although he managed to get himself a career – in an office somewhere where there was little contact with new people – his bent back and short legs and bald patch remained his eternal concern. He was convinced that everyone was struck on first meeting him by his disagreeable appearance. Even family and colleagues, he was sure, who saw him every day, never ceased to be amazed by his looks.

—He ought to get a dose of chemotherapy if he wants to know how bad it can get.

—In your case, not so bad at all.

The ugly man made it his life's work to improve his physical appearance. This was in the days before fitness lounges and health clubs, so he wasn't as lucky as we are today. Instead, he went swimming every day in the public baths to try and straighten out his back and lose his handlebars. He spent every penny he earned on lotions and cologne, hair restorers and conditioners, on smart suits and shirts of every colour until he found one which made his skin look less ruddy and matched his eyes. He went to the most expensive barbers, grew a beard which he got professionally groomed three times a week, commissioned a cobbler to make him special platform shoes, and got his tailor to cut his trousers a little long so you wouldn't notice. He replied to every ad in every newspaper which promised a better physique, or taught you how to improve your carriage.

Eventually, all this began to work. His family and his

colleagues commented on how well he looked. They would urge him to go out and find himself a lady friend. After all, he was getting on now. But he'd reply, not yet. The man's hair, which in his younger days was a dull, sandy colour and very fine, had, by the time he was in his forties, turned into a dazzling silver. It grew thicker too, and although all the hair restorer he had piled on year after year had never got rid of his bald patch, his hair was now thick and lustrous enough for him to comb it over successfully. His face, which used to have a vacant expression, now, with a few well-defined lines around the eyes and the mouth, gave him an intelligent, smiling look. So when Morag saw him again, far from thinking what an ugly wee man, she thought he looked quite handsome.

—Did he finally find himself a woman, then?

—Don't know. Next time Morag saw him was at his funeral. He was laid out in his coffin in his best suit and, with the hint of makeup the embalmers had put on him, he looked extremely elegant. She says he was quite the handsomest and most dashing corpse you'd ever seen.

For the first time in the nigh on three months she'd been in here, Paris laughed. Geraldine started laughing too, and in a moment the pair of them were killing themselves, neither really knowing why. Paris laughed until her eyes filled with fresh, new tears that dribbled bitterly into the corners of her mouth.

That night, Paris had trouble getting to sleep. Bloody moon. You'd think, wouldn't you, that with only two more days to go and the doctors and Morag and everyone all happy with her progress, and Paris herself feeling better with each passing day, that that moon would know the game was up? But no. It's got to keep on looming down on her, keep on pushing away at its bars, trying to escape so that it can engulf her completely. Every time she shut her eyes, there it was, big and blatant and swollen like a tumour. Even remembering her mum's explanation merely held it at bay, didn't make it recede. One thing worked, though. Always did. She gets run over. Imagines she gets run over by a truck. That obliterates the moon bugger all right.

A SCARY THOUGHT TO GET OTHER SCARIER THOUGHTS OUT OF YOUR HEAD

The road has a series of sharp edges which you can't see. It looks smooth enough to the naked eye, but it's ripping my flesh, slashing my shins into neat rashers, cutting so finely and cleanly that there's no blood, no pain, just rashers like I've been caught in a slicing machine for mountain ham. I seem to be caught by a necklace or something I'm wearing or the buttons of my blouse. Whatever, it must have got itself hooked on to the exhaust or some other protruding part of the undercarriage, and aligned me perfectly for the tarmac blades below me. Nor is it showing any sign of breaking, if anything it's pulling me up, tangling me into some moving part of the engine above my head. The noise from up there, the closer I'm pulled towards it, sounds less and less like a sooty, smoky grind, striking an even tenor, perfect pitch, soothing almost. I'm being pulled along backwards, my head to the front of the lorry, which from this position still appears to be travelling at a fair lick. But some whirlpool motion, precipitated perhaps by the spinning of two sets of massive tyres at either side of me, is causing my hair to be blown back into my face, and upwards towards the rotating, moving parts above me. Single strands of hair are getting sucked up like spaghetti into that black hungry mouth over my head, others spinning round the axle of the wheel nearest me at my left-hand side. Each hair resists for a second and then is torn out, popping out of my head, like that bubbly packaging I used to like puncturing between my fingers when I was a child. The sensation is invigorating, overriding the clatter and grime and grinding, pretty little polyps of pain, like tiny refreshing holes in the head. My body's been howked round somehow, and in the last moments before blackness, I can see out from under the vehicle, beyond the wheels to the street. People have noticed, they stand motionless, pointing at me, but not saying anything. Only, their faces have been panel-beaten into petrified revulsion, not pity or fear but helpless disgust. It occurs to me that this is the way they have always really looked at me. I don't want them looking at me. I don't want anyone to know about this. Then suddenly the road is no longer an evenly spread splicer, but is zigzagging crazily below me. Something gives above me, slackening me off. I hit the ground. Cool blackness. Can't see a thing. All I know is that I'm in pain, total pain in every part of me. All I know is that I'm in pain and that I'm in a mess. That's all, I'm just in a bloody mess.

Well, it's a bit of a sledgehammer to crack a nut, but that moon needs serious cracking. Maybe the cure seems worse than the illness, but then so's radiotherapy and chemotherapy and all that shit. Fact of the matter is, it does the trick. That moon backs off like nothing on earth. Revolted, outdone at its own game. Paris gets forty winks.

And wakes up feeling relaxed. Dreamy. She's that way

all day, while Morag flutters around her. She can't keep her attention on what Morag's saying, but then she never could. She makes sure, though, that she *looks* as though she's on the ball, nodding away at Morag or whoever else comes by to do whatever it is they're doing to her. Fine by her. Tomorrow. Or is it the day after? Mustn't lose count, lose the place. She'll check later if this is Tuesday or Wednesday. Must be Wednesday. Surely.

Morag's in a foul mood. Reason she wasn't here yesterday was because of her mother again. Morag's mother's not well. From the sound of it, she hasn't been well for donkey's years.

—What about your dad, Morag?

—Died. A long time ago.

—Sorry. What's wrong with your mother?

—Nerves. She's a nervous wreck. She was mugged.

—That's terrible.

—Can't cope now.

—No wonder. Is there no one else can help? Or is it just you in the family?

—There is someone else, but I don't dare contact him.

—Why not?

—My mother'd go mad.

—Who is he? Your brother? Uncle? What?

—Anyway, he lives too far away.

Morag was about to leave and tend to another of her charges, when she turned back.

—Paris?

—Yeah?

—You shouldn't let people lie to you.

—OK.

—When people lie to you, you *know*. Don't you? You kind of know inside.

—Who lied to you, Morag?

—Doesn't matter. It was you I was thinking of.

Paris dozed off and on. Not tired exactly. Not the sickness tired. Just relaxed and dreamy and sleepy. Maybe they'd given her something to control the excitement of getting out tomorrow. She tried to think about all the people she was about to be reunited with. Get herself psyched up for being with them again. Really *with* them. Not just the object around which they sat, her mum and dad and Colin and odd relatives and friends, but a person again.

Especially Simon. It'd be five weeks now since she'd cast eyes on him. She'd banned him from visiting when her hair, her lovely hair, gold from all the honey smiles poured upon her little head, had begun to fall out in handfuls and clumps. Every day since, he'd faithfully sent her a card, or a note, sometimes a long letter. He left books and magazines at the hospital reception, phoned regularly to talk to her – until this last fortnight when she'd banned even that. Tomorrow, after this good, long rest she was having, she was going to wow him. Doll herself up, be the old, sparkling, mad-hat, daring Paris again.

He'd never wavered for a moment, to the best of her knowledge, since this whole episode had started. Even her mum and dad had finally taken to him. Way back at the start of the sickness, it was Simon who kept insisting that there was something wrong, seriously wrong, that the doctors were fannying about, that they should *do* something. He knew before Paris did. He could have got out then, seen what was coming.

Didn't, though. Never wavered once. Leastways, not in front of her, or on the phone to her. Even when she put him through hell.

—Mister Bloody Nice Guy. But tell us, Si – just what option do you have? Not much you can do really *but* play the saint, is there? How does one go about telling his girlfriend of six years, Sorry, a wasting and potentially fatal disease isn't really what I'm looking for, so I think we ought to be seeing less of each other? Cancers don't really lend themselves to cooling-off periods, do they? You're just stuck with it, mate.

Jesus. She'd make it up to him. She'll sleep with him, that's what she'll do. Soon as poss. Should've slept with him way before now. Instead of all that silly prancing around naked in front of him. How immature she was. There was her, thinking, What a favour I'm doing this lad, letting him in on the secret of my happy little body. He must've been gagging for it the whole time. Still he'd kept his cool. Real gentleman, that Simon. She'd *wanted* to sleep with him. From the very first moment she'd got off with him, fifth year school. Maybe even more than he wanted to do it with her. She'd just always felt that something terrible would go wrong. She remembered Mum telling her, when she confessed about getting pregnant with Paris before she was married, that ever since, she'd worried herself silly about being punished.

Things were always supposed to get better. That was the deal. Better and better. Exponentially so. That was the deal Dad had made with her when she was a wee girl. Everything'd started off badly. Mum pregnant before they were married. Dad laid off. No Parisian honeymoon. But

—But from the moment you were born, Princess, things started to get better.

It was true, they did. Dad got a job. Not much. In an office. But soon he got promoted. They saved every penny, he and Mum, so that they could buy the flat in posh Dudhope Road. Then along came Colin, and that made things better still. Dad got more and more promotions and soon the pressure was off, financially. Still couldn't afford Paris – the real Paris – but had brilliant brilliant holidays all round the Scottish coastline. Mucking around the rockpools, looking for crabs; swimming in the rain. And all those honey smiles being poured over her pretty little head.

—You brought us luck. I'm telling you: in this house, things only ever get better and better. Deal?

—Deal.

And they shook hands on it when she was about six, and now she'd let them all down so so badly.

Trays came and went, and nurses flitted by like spirits, and once, Mum and Dad were beside her. But they agreed that, if they didn't mind, she'd save her energy tonight. At one point she thought she saw Simon, but she must've been dreaming. Si didn't go breaking the rules like that. The moon was around, somewhere in the back of her eye. She couldn't really see it, focus on it, but it was there, scaring her. Keep her mind on tomorrow. Getting out. Remember what Mum had said to her about the moon. Where it came from, how it started, how it was all her – Mum's – fault. How it wasn't real.

She wasn't yet two years old. Colin had just arrived. A girny baby. Mum and Dad were tired, had turned the telly up loud to cover his constant cries.

—Not something we did all the time, her mum said, worried, guilty. —Just that one night, we needed a rest. We were at our wits' end, weren't we, Brian?

As it turned out, Colin had fallen asleep straight away. It was Paris who woke up. The moon must have been at its lowest point in its elliptical cycle, and it must have been a clear night. To any adult out in the street it would have been a beautiful vision, the Sea of Tranquillity and the ragged edges of lunar mountains clearly visible. But to Paris, trapped behind the bars of her cot, never having seen anything so huge and bright at night before, it was terrifying.

—It took a neighbour to let us know. I'll never live it down.

The woman upstairs had been listening to her screams for two hours solid, and finally chapped on the McFarlane door to let them know that one of their kids was bawling its head off.

—You should've seen the look on her face. I half expected her to report us.

Paris was beside herself in that cot, kicking madly against the bars, all cried out, hoarse, panicking, when they finally released her, and Dad closed the curtains.

So that was all her moon was: a yellow moment of parental neglect. Just that, and it had jaundiced so many of her nights, tacked itself on to her sickness, exhibited itself in hookers' thighs, discharged its waxy light in the space between Paris and Simon. And now it was loitering somewhere at the back of her eyes. Or perhaps it was all around her now, casting this dank, ochre light throughout the ward. Or maybe that was just the hospital lighting.

Whatever, she'd beaten that moon before, and she'd do it again. Now that it'd come back, had waited for a moment of weakness, allied itself with her sickness, formed a cabal with the secret white cells that amassed themselves like gunpowder in her veins. Well, this was its last stand. Tomorrow – wasn't it tomorrow yet? She was sure Mum and Dad and Colin and maybe even Simon had all been back yet again. Must be time up.

She noticed it was dark outside. Sooner than she expected. She'd lost a whole day, thinking, dreaming, dozing. She wanted to sleep and, though she felt very tired, she couldn't stop her mind going round in circles. The G/god question kept coming up. In The Beginning There Was The Word And The Word Was Made Flesh. G/god knows what that's all about. And In The Beginning, too, There Was Nothing And Nothing Imploded Upon Itself. That took every bit as much a leap of faith. She'd had it with Science, science. Nothing the White Coats ever did with their Evil humming machines had saved the day. Her recovery had nothing to do with cytotoxins and sinister rays and fast-dividing cells. None of that had made a scrap of difference. It was the Honey Smiles and Paris in April; it was the Historic Deal that Everything would get Better and Better. It was the single Leaf on her red red Tree, serrated like a spinning blade, encrusted in blood. It was Simon Si naked Simon, turning away, blushing, when her body provoked a reaction in his that he thought shameful and she, wonderful.

Morag was at her side. She seemed upset about something. Probably her mother again. Said something about it being her birthday. Well, that shouldn't make her cry, should it? Paris had no energy to ask her what was the matter. But now Morag was saying something about tomorrow. Something about not worrying too much if it doesn't work out. About staying here a while longer with her, with Morag and Geraldine and all her friends.

Shit, she hadn't, had she? Morag hadn't screwed up her release? She couldn't be sure. Morag was too upset and Paris was too done in to try and work out what was happening. Whatever, she'd fight all the way to make sure she got out tomorrow. In the morning, once she'd got a proper sleep, Paris'd be up with the lark and shouting the odds if anyone tried to keep her in this dump.

Had to get some sleep. Sleepsleepsleep. The Scary

Thought was too exhausting. Instead, try another old favourite. Think about

HER LAST DAY AT HOME

—See if anyone ever asked me, like in those magazine questionnaires, where's your favourite place in the whole wide world, and famous people always say St Mark's in Venice or Old Town Square in Prague, I'd say this street.

She'd been sitting at the bay window and it was bright but not sunny. Early January. Dad was drinking his tea and reading the paper, pretending it was a normal day. Mum sewing something. Colin had made himself scarce, having hugged her, surprisingly, before finding an important reason for going out.

—I'd have thought you'd have said Paree, Dad said, smiling over the top of his paper.

—And my favourite journey would be from the top of the Drive there at the shops, all the way down to the park at the bottom.

No one replied, so she recited to herself the names of all the trees she had managed to find out. Sweet chestnut, hawthorn, the gorgeous lemony laburnum outside the old brothel at number 26. All of them broadleaf, like her street was some nature reserve somewhere and not smack in the middle of a big smoky city. She knew which trees the grey squirrels preferred. She could recognise, among the many that had taken up residence of late, which were her magpies, the ones that had always been there.

Then she heard herself say,

—If anyone is going to ask me, they'd better get a move on.

Which was a bit spiteful, but she wished they wouldn't sit there pretending it was a day like any other. She heard

Dad's newspaper rustling shut. Him getting up out of his chair and leaving the room. From beyond the closed door she could hear the murmur of tears percolating in his eyes, listened to them flow and gush like a river in spate. She heard her mum's footsteps behind her.

—Heck of a turn-up for the books this, eh?

Best she could do. She turned her knees to one side, and patted her lap. Paris sat down. Twenty-one years old. Ridiculous. Mum put her arm around her daughter's shoulder and pulled Paris's shaking head towards her. The last day in her own house, beside her window, the Red Tree casting a crimson shadow on them both. And her mum's shoulder, clenched up with despair, relaxed as Paris lay her head upon it. A Mother and Child *pietà*. Used to be she could fit snugly on her mum's knee, her whole child's body curled up between lap and shoulder. She'd be too big now. But, then, a funny thing happened, that last day in her lovely house, before the ambulance came. Her mum's shoulder grew as Paris placed her head upon it. Her whole body grew in girth and Paris's became smaller. She could feel herself diminish, fade, and she huddled up close the way she used to when she was four.

—Everything's going to be fine, love.

—I know, Mum.

And Paris believed her. Still did, as she fell asleep in her hospital bed with nurse Morag Simms holding her hand and crying and asking Paris to stay in tomorrow, help old Morag celebrate her fortieth birthday.

SEVEN

She woke early. Very early, because there were no nurses bustling around, noising people up for their various tests and bed baths before breakfast. Every other patient was asleep. She'd snapped awake, Paris. No pain and feeling better than she'd felt in an age. She swung her legs out the side of her bed, yawned and stretched and felt that the last couple of days' rest had made all the difference in the world. Friday 17 March 1997 at last. Unless Morag had stuck her oar in right enough and had made them keep her in.

One way to find out: start packing up, getting dressed, see if anyone obstructs her. She decided to have a shower. She looked out her washbag and found a Safeway bag with clean undies in it – a sign everything was going to plan. Mum must've brought them last night, for the big Homecoming. A newly washed dress in there too. Perfect.

Off she tottered in the direction of the bathroom. Nobody stirred. She glanced back to check out the nurses' glass office. Geraldine in there, drowsing.

The shower was brill. Great to have her body uncovered, free of the clammy sheets and sticky nightgown that'd been getting into a fankle and riding up around her bum, tangling her up for weeks now. The water skooshed out fast and hot and so noisy she waited for Geraldine to come running in and tell her to turn it off, she'd wake the whole ward. But no one came, and for the first time in weeks she was by herself. No one knew where she was or what she was doing. Like a real person. She turned the water up as fast and as hot as she could take it, almost scalding herself. The jets of steaming shower were like needles, but needles that respected the integrity of her body, didn't insist on breaking through her skin into the privacy of what lay beneath. Water bounced off her eyelids and lips, squelched through her thin hair, skelped her shoulders, babbled noisily in her mouth and nostrils and ears, cascaded down her sides and legs. Head held back, she turned around and around on the spot in a silent dance. Surprised that her body was solid enough to impede the water from pouring right through her. Last few weeks, it was like she was becoming invisible, fading away to nothing, rays and lasers passing through her as though she wasn't there.

She looked at herself when she came out. Bony. Her tummy, instead of sticking its wee head out to welcome the world, still burrowed itself inside her. Her legs were like sticks; arms and fingers, rakes. In the sheet of dull tin that served for a mirror in the bathroom her eyes were definitely still a little sunken. But there was a brightness in them, and a sheen to her skin that hadn't been there before. Not for a long while. A liveliness, almost healthy. She rubbed her head energetically with the towel, her scalp still a bit raw, but at long last there was enough hair there to merit a proper rubbing. Clean and talcumed, she brushed her teeth and virtually no blood appeared. Usually, the sink looked like a slaughterhouse floor even after the most gingerly of brushings, but this morning she gave them a right good going-over and there was only the odd speck. Paris leant over the basin and swayed to the feel of air flowing round her, cooling her still-damp back, freshening between her thighs, chilling her scalp. Her legs and arms might be thin, but she felt their power returning, felt solid and supported, almost muscly.

She felt like whistling when she came out of the shower, but remembered the sleeping, dying patients. So she took exaggerated tiptoes like she used to do when she was a kid to make people laugh. She sat on her bed, wiggling a little in the cleanness of her new knickers and bra, smoothed out her dress and pulled it on.

Yellow knee-length dress, rounded, buttoned neck, sleeves to the elbow. It looked nice, but what Paris really revelled in was being covered up. Covered by something she wanted to be covered in, of her own choosing. Some kind of control, at last. Weeks and weeks of being exposed when she didn't want to be exposed, of loose nightgowns and sheets holding nothing in, stripping themselves away from her like pimps showing off their wares. Her body playing peek-a-boo with every passing stranger. Now she could define her own contours. Erect a boundary between herself and the rest of the world. These are my limits, and beyond these borders ye shall not pass unless I bleeding well say so. She'd never thought a simple sale-bought dress could be so respectable and respectful. Once on, and straightened out, patted down, she was, for the first time in months, Paris McFarlane. Person.

No shoes. Shit. Mum and Dad'll've thought she won't

need them, thought she'd be wheeled from door to door. Not today. No way. Then her eye caught Morag standing beside her, dangling a pair of shoes in her hand.

—I thought they could do with a bit of a shine. Can't have a Paris looking like she's been scuffing her way round Maryhill, can we?

Then, Morag looked unhappy, almost tearful.

—I'm going to miss you, Paris.

—Come off it. I've been a right royal pain in the ass. Especially to you.

Morag tried to laugh.

—You're an angel compared to some of them in here.

Paris turned around to start packing again, and asked if it would be all right if she phoned home. She'd do it down at the entrance, get a breath of fresh air while she was at it. Morag didn't answer, just kept on looking sadly at Paris's bed, as though Paris herself were still in it. Paris shrugged and headed off for the lifts, newly polished shoes click-clacking on the lino.

It was cold outside the main door. Paris breathed in deeply. Stale exhaust, River Kelvin wafting coconut-scented spring gorse down from the hills, steely Clyde with its backdraught of brackish sea water. Maybe it was because she'd been cooped up for so long that her nose seemed especially receptive this morning, but she could swear that amidst that medley of notes there was the definite red tang of her Tree. If she'd dropped dead right there, right at that moment, she'd have died happy.

Then she had an idea. Instead of waiting here for Mum and Dad to come and get her, she'd slip off home now. Surprise them. Dudhope was a fifteen-minute walk away. In her condition, make that half an hour. But: she'd left her hair upstairs. And she only had a skimpy summer dress on. And it was March, cold. She was about to head back, when she laughed, realised she was already down the drive, out the hospital gates, and walking up Dumbarton Road.

Stepping along in the cold spring sun, Paris told herself one of Morag's old tales that she'd always rather liked.

THE MAN WHO DIDN'T GO HOME TO DIE

There was a man, in a ward that Morag used to work on, who had terminal cancer or something. It was decided to let him go home and be cared for by his wife and three daughters and two sons. A Macmillan nurse would come in on a regular basis and they worked out a cocktail of painkillers that could be strengthened as the cancer got more painful. The man lived in some big fuck-off house (the description Paris's, not Morag's original) overlooking some bonnie wee loch in quiet Milngavie. All in all, as serene and as pleasant a death you could wish for.

But on the appointed day for his transfer from hospital to house, the man had somehow or other made his own way out of the hospital and was nowhere to be found when his Salvation Army of a family trooped by to get him. A hunt went up for the old scoundrel, but there was no word of him, until a week later when a woman went to the police to say he was in her flat, dead. Made the papers and everything.

What had happened was, this old geezer, knocking on seventy, a businessman of some sort, elder in the church, had decided against his prearranged idyllic death, surrounded by his loved ones, overlooking his bonnie wee loch. Decided against his doting wife and devoted offspring's prospectus: bed and record player and bookshelf rigged up in the conservatory because he was big on his garden and Verdi and the Bible; old friends all organised to come round on a strict rota, no more than two visitors a day, for half an hour each, max., lest they tire him unduly. They'd cooked up a menu, with the doctors' blessing, for soups and purées according to his tastes, and malt whiskies (peaty Islays, his faves) to take the sting out of the medicines. But the blighter throws all this over and instead, with no medication on him, buses it across town to the east, risks life and limb negotiating the mean streets, and knocks on the door of Carrie-Ann, a prostitute of whom he had been a regular client.

Now there's a decision for you. Two decisions: for he's straight with Carrie-Ann and tells her he's about to kick it, and could he stay there until he does, and she says yes! He had no money on him and, unless some transaction had taken place before, it seems Carrie-Ann is living proof that there is such a thing as a tart with a heart. Which is pretty damn unlikely in this impoverished city. He wants to die next to her, with her red-and-black frillies on (on her or him, Paris wasn't sure). The evening paper ran the story for a few weeks, and Carrie-Ann swore the old rascal managed to get it up and do the biz on several occasions before he finally copped it. She was tight-lipped (Morag'd said, no doubt innocently) about any financial understanding that they may have come to. Certainly one way of saving your loved ones from grieving: the poor widow and fatherless children were hopping blazing mad. Good riddance to bad rubbish, said one of the sons to the paper, despite the old guy having been allegedly up till then an exemplary father. The sad bit was that, turns out he didn't die in flagrante delicto, but while Carrie-Ann was out on the rounds, making poppy for groceries to feed two.

Just imagine. The story intrigued Paris for the first two weeks of her hospital term. There *he* is, in surely excruciating pain, but still on the job; there *she* is, with some old guy on top of her whose stiffness could at any given moment spread further than was technically necessary. What must it have felt like, that night, when he finally expired, alone in the manky flat of a user, halfway up a grim high-rise, knowing no one, his hired love out on the streets and no doubt shooting up? Wasn't love. Not even of the normal physical type: he was no Sean Connery to whom age had been kind. In the mugshots in the paper, he looked a hundred years old. Nor had life been kind in that sphere to poor ravaged Carrie-Ann. Wasn't penance: from what Carrie-Ann said, he enjoyed every minute his pain would allow him. What, then? Perhaps he reckoned hell would be better than heaven. Maybe he felt he just couldn't die as saintly as his family wanted. Maybe Carrie-Ann expected nothing of him at a time when he had nothing left to give.

Who knew? Each time she thought of it, the story either delighted Paris, or made her shudder. Maybe it was true, and maybe it wasn't, who knew?

And who cared, because right then, halfway along Dumbarton Road, Paris forgot all about the Man Who Didn't Go Home To Die, suddenly realising she was in Gay Paree. Not really, but almost. Through the morning stillness all around, like the air itself was dozing, you could hear the beginnings of morning noises. Shops opening up, milk lorries rattling, engines revving. Reminded her of her school French book. *Monsieur Dupont* opening up his *boulangerie*, *Mademoiselle Vérité* cycling – *en bicyclette* – along Dumbarton Road. There's accordion in the air, whiffs of breeze scatting around her. *Celui-là!* – dirty great Partick Cross has gone all Place de la République just for her benefit.

Then she was at the foot of Policy Road, the hill that propped up her very own special little world. Up there near the clouds, where the gardens and the insolent little apple blossom and her shady red lady of a tree got the best of the air, nearest the sun. Halfway up and she could see the high sycamores and elms. The laburnums around the old playpark, their baby golden cascades beaming like honey smiles. The threadbare poplars shivering, skinny, over the kids' home. A big chestnut behind the house that everyone said used to be a brothel. Three-quarters up she had to stop for a breather. She sat there for a few moments and said sorry to her body for working it so hard. Don't take the huff with me again now. I know your tantrums. From now on, we're in this together. Spend quality time together. Pig out on Simon. And she felt her blood gurgling through her veins, her heart thumping in agreement.

Then she heard them coming. Voices, footsteps, people coming her way. Colin first, jangle-nerved as usual, trying to rush up the pace. Then Mum, then Dad, then Simon. They hadn't seen her.

Poor Mum – she'd aged ten years in as many weeks. But, kick a spray of Troon sea water over her and she'd plump up lovely, like a Clyde Valley cherry. Dad'll be a pushover: just a smile and a sly reach for his hand'll do the trick. Next thing he'll be pretending he's got something in his eye; walk ahead.

But it was Simon who saw her first. Then Colin, Dad. Last, Mum. They were looking disbelieving, screwing up their eyes, hands over their brows as if she was miles away, not just a block and a half over the brow of Policy Road. Once she got closer, she'd treat them to the biggest smile she had – a honey smile in repayment for all the honey smiles that had brought her to this point, through everything, coming out winning. She raised her arms, and they felt longer, more sinewy, thanks to the loss of body fat. There was vigour in them now, and she let them fly in majestic sweeps through the air, unfurling. She was almost running, loving the pulling at her ligaments, the elasticity of muscle and skin and joints. They were waving back, Simon making a dash for her, Dad close on his heels, Colin punching the air. Mum's stood dead still, everything about her in temporary paralysis, except for her eyes, which even from here Paris can see are polished in tears and thanksgiving and consummate love.

Paris had never felt so light. Her steps like an athlete's, sailing up that steep slope. She could still hear the echo of Nurse Morag Simms' voice in the background, asking her not to go, not to leave her, and Paris felt so sorry for that big, sad nurse, stuck back there in her sullen hospital. Here, now, a sudden wind bossa-novas sea-saltily up from the Clyde below, funnelling up the hill. And there's so little of Paris left these days, she's hoisted right up off her feet, so that she's lying flat out on the breeze. Dad'll think she's slipped, panic she'll come down with a thud. But she knows she won't. She'll float down like a feather, pillowed by the puffs of piccolo breeze. All she can see now is transparent cloud, wispy cirrus as thin and as bright as her own poor hair. And she catches sight of the moon. A pretty little sexy blue moon, half hidden behind a fold of cloud, like a young healthy woman's breast, pressing against a lacy-white robe.

But she's tired now. She's going to need them to catch her after all. Which they will. They will. At the last moment, a squall of sadness comes over her. Shame she'll not be able to give them all that big honey smile she'd promised herself.

EIGHT

No one knows the hell she's been through. All anyone ever sees is that big happy smile, her blonde, sunny exterior and thinks, Not much up with that one. Like the man from the library who's standing in front of her now, behind his desk, bracing himself for his weekly dose of compulsory cheerfulness as he checks her *Life and Times of Mary Queen of Scots* through.

She's saying:

—Got a taste for biogs this weather, haven't I? Field Marshal Montgomery last week. Monty. Never finished that one. Got as far as the desert bit and began to feel sand in uncomfortable places, the way you do.

She smiles and that's all the library man sees, a big smiling woman. And she laughs, and that's all he hears, an overfriendly, overweight customer who talks too much. What he doesn't know, can't hear, is that inside, all the time she's chatting away to him, she's thinking to herself: Fuckwit.

Admittedly, she's more out of sorts today than usual, but that's not why she's thinking the library man's a Fuckwit. She always thinks that. Every Saturday morning that she's been coming in here for the last year she's considered the man lacking in the most basic courtesies. He doesn't so much listen to you as hear you out. She knows fine he wants shot of her a.s.a.p., so she makes a point of talking politely about this and that for a good few minutes with him every week. It's a recently acquired habit, this going to the library, spending the best part of the week with a new book. Not going to let some little Fuckwit of a library man ruin it for her.

She stumbled on the term Fuckwit quite by accident and liked it immensely. Morag picks up swearwords like street-sweepers pick up litter, spearing the words in mid-air, as they float from mouth to foul mouth. She likes to think of herself as cleaning the atmosphere of these poisonous little sounds; storing them up For Internal Use Only. Just as an incinerator burns up filth and waste to generate light and heat, Morag's little internal combustion engine of expletives and insults fuels the outwardly plump, cheery Mrs Simms. Powers that hefty body through the day.

Which is not to say that Morag is soft on swearing. She most certainly is not. She is revolted by these words in their audible state. She's doing the world a favour, taking a few of the vile things out of circulation; putting them to good, private use.

She waves goodbye to the library man, and continues on her Saturday morning rounds, hobbling on her worn-down shoes but the only pair she'll wear, smiling as if nothing were the matter. Making her way down the busy shopping street, she nods and talks to shopkeepers and assistants, waves to acquaintances, strikes up mini-conversations with strangers and generally goes about her business in a bright and practical way. That's how she is, Morag: sunny on the outside, crisp and efficient underneath. Or rather, that's how she should be, and will be again. Everyone agreed she was a most efficient staff nurse for years. Good at Getting Things Done.

Now that she no longer has to Get Things Done, apart from her own Things, she can afford to be a little more sunny than efficient for a change. If, on the inside, she is calling half the world Pricks, Arseholes and Twats, that's only for the sake of equilibrium. One has to keep oneself in balance. Too much sunniness isn't good for anyone. Calling folk what she really thinks of them, into herself, is Morag's way of keeping things stabilised.

Dumbfuck. There's another new one. Heard that in the street a few months ago. A young couple and that's the kind of words they were using to each other. Morag just despised the pair of them. Stupid hairstyles and much too loud and draped over each other like they were laughing at the rest of the world for not being young and slim and confident.

—Your old man's just a total Dumbfuck, the young man said to his sweetheart, and Morag grimaced, scooped the offending word clean up out of the air, confiscated it.

So now the woman in the chemist's, sixty if she's a day and more makeup on her face than on her counter, is a Dumbfuck. So's the stupid policeman who's directing the traffic because the lights at the Cross are out again. She keeps a determinedly patient smile on her lips and friendliness in her tone of voice when she's dealing with the badly educated just-out-of-school girl at the flower stall when she stops to pick up her weekly bunch for Mother, consoling herself all the time by thinking quietly: Ugly Little Retard. And all those who supposedly organise buses in this armpit of a city are all Dumbfucks and Dickheads, as she taps her foot waiting at the stop.

She would think these things any day of the week. But, as of late last night when his plane got in, the Dumbest and Fuckest of all the people in the whole stupid world was undoubtedly Mister William bloody Grant.

All she did was write him a letter. All she needed was a letter in return. If that. The *last* thing she expected was for him to hightail it halfway across the world and land on her doorstep.

Or rather, The Devon. Just about the most expensive hotel in town. He'd stay there for a whole week and then, should he decide to stay on a bit longer, he intended to find himself a more reasonably priced hotel, or even a flat to rent. God forbid it comes to that.

It was all her fault. She should never have sent that letter. She tried to explain, when he'd written back to her, that he should've just ignored it. She tried again, when he phoned last month. And even last night she'd tried to suggest that they didn't bother meeting up, that he stay for a few days, see Loch Lomond or whatever, and go home without bothering either her or her mother. She hadn't been well last year when she wrote that silly letter. Not well at all. She just had to tell someone about what she thought she'd seen, and William was the furthest away. It didn't matter too much if he thought her mad or not. But she was on the mend now and she realised the folly of writing to him, inviting him over. Couldn't he please forget the whole episode?

She'd written to him in Windhoek, Namibia, before she'd realised she *was* ill. Just after that girl died on her last year. When she thought she saw her again, on the top of Policy Road hill. During the same period she was having a difficult time with her mother. Thought she'd seen *her* up there too. And the boy. The three of them rising up off the top of the hill, floating off into the clouds.

Morag had suffered a little nervous trouble in the past. Was never anything in particular that'd caused it. On that occasion, just silly things coming together at the same time. The situation with her mother'd been bad for years, ever since the assault. And although she was an experienced nurse who naturally'd seen plenty of folk die, the McFarlane girl's passing hit Morag badly for some reason. All of that smack bang between her fortieth birthday and the fifteenth anniversary of her divorce. No wonder she saw folks ascending off pavements, getting sucked up into big, blank, dirty clouds.

She'd tried to explain to Mr Grant that her letter was out of character, a wee cry for help, in the wrong direction. She shouldn't have written it and she didn't need help any more. His arrival, really, would only make matters worse. Set her back.

—I assure you, Mrs Simms, I haven't the slightest intention of making a nuisance of myself.

Terribly rah-rah, his voice on the phone. Dignified. Recognisably South African. Like someone had flattened out his vowels with a rolling pin. She felt she was talking to the President of some far-off country. You tend to think that in faraway places there's nobody but presidents and soldiers, maybe some poor people, because that's all you ever see on the telly, or in the paper. Morag had to fight against calling him 'Sir' all the time.

She ought to be proud, really – three men in her life, all of them such big shots. None of them round here would have guessed that Morag's own father was once a Member of Parliament. Not the library man nor the flower shop girl nor half her patients back in the ward before she went on the sick, nor any of the other Fuckwits out there. Not herself, to be honest. Had very little memory of him being an MP. Remembered him more after he'd resigned. When he was around the house, the ordinary house.

Then there was Michael. Another VIP. Well, almost. Her husband, legally, of precisely three years, and in reality, of less than one. Fifteen years ago now. He'd done well since. Good luck to him. Never did her any harm. She probably never even loved him, actually. She told her counsellor that what she had wanted back then was to be married. To Michael. In that order. What she did love though were the gadgets Michael picked up all the time. Theirs was one of the first houses to have a video recorder – one of those old Beta ones – a microwave oven, low-energy lightbulbs that saved a fortune but made even the brightest of sunny evenings feel like gloomy December. Years after they'd split up, he phoned her. Not to ask how she was getting on, but to tell her he was phoning from a mobile. She was, he said, thirty-third on his list of hundreds to whom he was delivering the exciting message.

Michael foresaw the future, no two ways about it. He couldn't actually *make* anything himself but he bought bits of computers from all over the world, hired people who could fit them together, and sold the assembled articles just when word processors were becoming all the rage. Made himself a fortune, by all accounts. But that was after he'd left her. Discontinued her, had upgraded and moved on. Unless someone comes up with another new-fangled form of communication, likelihood is she'll never hear from him again.

Last but not least was good old William Grant. She'd never met him – or rather, she must have, but she'd've been so young at the time. He was the biggest mystery of all. Like something out of a story. Distant, bigger than ordinary people, some kind of a dragon or wolf. Or a Fearsome King. It was amazing how, from so far away, he could have caused all those terrible things to happen. Such power.

And now look what she'd gone and done. She'd brought the Dragon over here. She hadn't meant to, because she wasn't herself at the time, but she'd let the bad man out of the story book. William Grant was arriving tonight. She was meeting him at his hotel. Heaven knows what havoc he'd wreak in the real world.

—Thank you, driver, she said politely as she got off at her stop, hanging on to the handrail for dear life as he braked viciously. Paki Dumbfuck.

Every time Morag gets off the bus at the stop in Highfield Road, she has to make a decision. Head for her own house, or her mother's? Her mother's up towards Kings' Drive, her own flat down the road towards the river? You could fit all of Morag's flat into the hall of her mother's. Originally the plan had been that Michael and she would move out of the little top-storey one-bedroomed flat after a couple of years and move into a flat not unlike her mother's. After that, she'd hoped for one of the semis like you get in Dudhope and the far end of Policy Road, or like Isobel Grant's in Bunnahabhain. Course, things turned out different. Michael could buy her a whole bloody street of semis these days, while she was still stuck four storeys up in a tenement. Perhaps she should try and get alimony or something out of him. Then again, she really rather liked her bright wee top-storey two-room-and-kitchen. And she didn't like making a nuisance of herself.

She couldn't face her mother today. Her mother'd know damn fine something was afoot; be on to Morag from the word go, know she was hiding something. She'd phone her later. For the moment, best keep quiet and calm until her meeting tonight. She headed down the hill, cut off left to get on to Policy Road.

—I'd forgotten about March, said William Grant.

He'd met her at his hotel entrance, asked her if she'd liked to dine and when she said No, had bought her a large brandy and insisted that the waiter clean the ashtray that was close to her, even though it wasn't dirty and she'd told him she didn't smoke. He asked her how she was and how her mother was, as though he was their bank manager or a neighbour: polite, but not terribly interested. Yet he must be interested. Else he wouldn't have travelled over six thousand miles to see them.

—Forgotten how grey they could be. March days. Don't they get you down, Mrs Simms?

They get a lot worse than this. Days when the clouds breathe down so heavily you could almost reach up and scrape flakes off them.

William Grant laughed: —Spring still as behind schedule every year as the trains and trams, is it?

—We don't have trams any more.

—Of course not. Although, they didn't get rid of them everywhere, you know. In some places, they've reintroduced them.

—Have they.

In the pictures Morag had seen of William Grant in the newspaper, he looked chubbier and sterner, shorter-haired, more like you'd think an Afrikaaner would look. Tighter-lipped. She'd always thought: Dour old Bastard. But the gentleman in front of her, sipping his fancy malt, was a reedy, wispy, not unpleasant-looking man for his age. Affable enough, a bit wishy-washy maybe, with his cufflinks and tiepin, wafting lavender all over the place. Not how she'd imagined a sorcerer would look. In conversation he was being a thorough gentleman, straining, though, to work the discussion round to the old days.

—Before I left, they were building whole new villages on the outskirts of the city. Did they ever finish them?

—The schemes.

—I've seen such developments in Lagos and Nairobi. Can't really imagine them here.

—I can't imagine them *not* being here.

He was trying hard to give the impression of being composed, surrounding himself with his big chair and his expensive whisky and fancy hotel. But from time to time, he'd shuffle a little in his seat, glance up at her. Morag was getting the hang of him, feeling with every moment a little less in awe of this African returnee.

—Your mother was a very keen advocate of the new estates, wasn't she?

—Was she?

This was not the mother she knew; she couldn't help him. But that was OK. She was beginning to realise that the less information she gave him, the more he wanted it. He changed the topic and ordered them both another drink. They spoke about hotels and service and how only the Americans knew how to do it, though in fact Morag's never been to America. After an awkward silence, he asked, tentatively, where the name Simms came from and Morag told him all about Michael and computers and lied and said that although they were separated now, they were still quite close. She also said that, yes she had a partner at the moment, but she didn't think she'd keep him on for long.

There'd been a time, from her mid-twenties to mid-thirties, when it had been important to her that people actually believed her little fictions. Now she made things up out of habit. She didn't really care if old man Grant believed her or not. She'd just prefer that he did.

—Your father died when you were quite young?

He blurted the question out when the waiter came with fresh drinks, as if he needed camouflage. Now he was getting closer to the knuckle. A tad too directly for Morag's taste but, after all, he had travelled all this distance to ask precisely these questions.

—I was about twelve.

She told him she didn't want to speak about her father. He nodded and they went back to mundane topics. In reality, she genuinely wasn't in the mood to talk about Dad – it could bring on her old trouble. But also, it suited her purposes to keep William hanging on a little while longer before giving away any real information.

What does he think she knows? That he and her mother were still a Big Secret? That they had been just Good Friends? He had no idea what was general knowledge this side of the world, and what was not. This might be his hotel and he was buying the drinks, but Morag was the one with all the trump cards. Just like she used to have, in the ward, when she was Staff Nurse Simms.

At 10.30 on the dot she made moves to go. She'd spent just over two hours in the company of the Evil Sorcerer. He'd turned out to be really quite charming and – so long as he didn't come into contact with Mother – quite harmless. The evening had gone much better than she could have imagined so best thing was to leave it at that for the moment.

He was disappointed, naturally. All they'd really done was exchange pleasantries and talk about trivia. Morag had started the evening nervous, feeling she'd been tricked into his lair. But she'd given away nothing. Instead, she'd found out that she had real power over the old geezer – the only one who could unlock the past for him. At the hotel door, while she was waiting for the taxi he'd ordered her, she spelt out firmly that under no circumstances was William to try to contact her mother. She'd have a heart attack if she knew that William Grant was in town. It'd set her back years. Bring on her arthritis, palpitations, the lot. Leave it to Morag to judge when and how the two old friends were to meet.

—I've thoroughly enjoyed your company tonight, Mrs Simms.

—Morag.

—Morag, he said, though he seemed unhappy about it.

—And you must call me William. You wouldn't be free again tomorrow night, by any chance?

—Lucky for you, William, I'm quite happy to keep a certain gentleman at bay at the moment, so, yes, I'd be delighted, thank you.

When the taxi arrived, William asked for the fare to be put on his account, and was about to close the taxi door for her, when he bent down and looked inside.

—Morag. Did you know my sister? Isobel Grant?

—Auntie Isobel?

Morag laughed quietly to herself when the taxi drew away. Prat. Auntie Isobel, indeed. He'd find out all about her soon enough. She asked the driver if he wouldn't mind going the long way round. Down to the river and up Policy Road. Her flat was only a ten-minute walk away. Had to make the ride worthwhile.

The taxi U-turned at the end of the street, came up and passed the hotel entrance again. She saw William Grant standing there – lean and lank, waving, turning and trailing his solitary way back inside. By all accounts, he was married. With children. Didn't seem the type. He looked like a loner. Perhaps, she thought, he's an impostor, then turned round in her seat, let out a little yelp of laughter. The driver smiled and asked if she'd had a good night out. Morag didn't reply.

Morag spent the best part of the next day mucking around the house. With the worry of William Grant's arrival she'd let things get into a state. Time she should've spent ironing and tidying up and mopping the kitchen floor, she'd spent sitting worrying and going out to get her hair done and eating. She made up for it today, though, and by the middle of the afternoon, her little home was spick and span. She thought she might even invite William over one of these evenings. For tea, perhaps. After all, it was a lovely little flat. Nothing to be ashamed of, even if he did live in a mansion or whatever. Morag's flat was bright and airy and tidy and afforded good views across the city.

She never phoned her mother. Her mother would certainly not phone her. That wasn't how it worked. Her mother'd hear the lie in her voice, the secret she was keeping from her, if she phoned home with some cock-and-bull story about why she hadn't called round; how she'd had a quiet night in last night. Morag'd get in touch tomorrow. See if there was a bit of housework for her to do. Tell her she'd been out in the morning with a couple of old friends from the hospital, then didn't feel well in the afternoon and'd gone straight to bed.

Morag went off and had a bath, looking forward to tonight's meeting with William. First Namibian she'd ever met. Rich one too. If she'd been working she'd've been able to tell the girls all about it. Regale them with stories of The Hotel Devon, and how her uncle'd invited her over to Namibia to live in his villa. Swimming pool and everything. Who knows – she might end up never coming back.

Tonight she'd accept his offer of a meal. Why not? No

reason he shouldn't pay for what Morag had to offer. It'd be nice spending a few days in the company of a man who found her life a subject of limitless fascination. He didn't give a tuppenny fuck about her herself, of course. So what? But everyone she grew up around – her mother, father, Grant's own sister – and what had happened to them was all hugely important to him. There was a gap in the old man's life, and Morag was the only one who could fill it. Might as well enjoy the ride while it lasts.

—It was her idea, and to be honest, it never really caught on.

They were dining at his hotel. One of the best places to eat in the whole country, they say, and certainly the soup was very nice. She'd ordered veal with orange and wild mushrooms for her second course and he was having spit-roast kidneys. Michael used to like taking her to nice Italian trattorias and gourmet curry houses, and she had treated her mother from time to time to lunch in the likes of Pierre Victoire and other good, competitively priced restaurants in town. This place, though, was in a different league.

—Was Isobel the auntie type?

Morag laughed: —Not really.

She'd hated Isobel Grant's guts. Scrawny witch of a woman under her Jaeger and Fraser's outfits. Morag's mother always said that Miss Grant wore better clothes than anyone she knew. Camel-hair coats, hats from John Lewis in Edinburgh. And all on no apparent income whatsoever.

The woman never smiled. She had this hard-bitten, angry look about her all the time. Even when she was trying to be nice and bending down to give you a shilling or a sweetie. Under her smile, you could hear the bones in her face crackling. Morag's father despised her, and her mother was scared of her. It was Isobel herself who suggested that Morag, when she was around six years old, should call her Auntie. They were in the street and her mother said, Of course, That'd be lovely, Wouldn't it, Morag? and Morag wasn't bothered one way or the other because, not already having any aunties, it didn't seem like a post of much distinction. Later, Mummy said she was never to call Miss Grant Auntie Isobel in front of Daddy.

—I was a little frightened of her myself.

He looked as if he might say more, and Morag waited politely. But he bent his head again to concentrate on his eating.

He waited a moment, then said: —Your father did well for himself, I hear. Elected to Westminster, no?

—He was an MP for less than one parliamentary term.

—You miss him.

She nodded.

—We all miss our fathers.

She was amazed that he could even remember having a father. Morag pretended to concentrate on her food, as she considered how to proceed. She could throw him off the scent again, change the subject, make him wait a little longer before giving anything away. Finally, she decided he'd waited long enough. Time to reward him with a few nuggets of information. She'd tell him everything eventually, of course. Bit by bit. There was plenty he didn't know, that was clear.

—They hated each other. My father and your sister.

—Did they.

It wasn't a question, and she didn't answer. He turned his eyes away from her and looked down at his plate. Like Morag's old patients, William just couldn't be sure just how much power the plump, smiling lady across the table from him had. He was making her realise for the first time that she was missing her job. It'd been nearly a year since her little breakdown and sitting here with William reminded her just how good she was at her work, how in control it'd made her feel. She was on the mend, Morag, for sure.

—His big theme in Parliament was the Permissive Society, did you know that?

—No. No I didn't.

—How the pill and homosexuality and pop music were debauching us all. He used to use *me* as an example. 'I have a little daughter,' he'd say. 'Morag. Six years old. The very soul of innocence. I don't want to see her corrupted.' Once, he even took a picture of me into the House. He was so proud of me, Daddy. Thought I was beautiful. And I think he was right – about the permissive society and queer folk and all of that. Don't you?

—I don't know.

—He accused Isobel of running a house of ill repute.

William put down his knife and fork, rubbed his eyes and took a deep breath.

—She ran a dating agency.

The waiter brought them their desserts. Morag got tucked into her chocolate rum soufflé, talking between mouthfuls, as though they were chatting about perfect strangers. William picked at his sorbets.

—As I understand it, from what Mother's told me, Isobel didn't bother her backside about Daddy's statements to the press and questions in the House about genteel depravity. Instead, she just let it quietly be known that, if indeed it was a house of ill repute she was running, then Mr Lapraik, MP himself had once paid into the establishment. And she had the bank statement to prove it.

Morag looked up from her soufflé, and smiled at the older man, said what a cool operator his sister was.

—I'm sorry, said William.

—Of course, he resigned his seat before there was too much of a fuss, so it could have been a lot worse. The local rag, though, got wind of it all. I looked it up in the library, a while back. They were asking questions about a cheque, made out simply to 'Grant. Bunnahabhain Road'. Five hundred pounds. Lot of money in those days.

—Please, Morag. You must tell your mother that I am here.

Morag, scraping her plate of the bitter-sweet chocolate, said: —Sorry, William. It's quite out of the question.

Her mother was in the bath. Morag was watering the plants around the house, most of them cuttings from originals that flowered gaily in her own bright top flat down the hill, but which struggled to survive in this big gloomy place. Last night, she'd felt as if William's secret visit was all going well, that she had it all under control. This morning, though, after seeing her mother, Morag realised just how thin the ice was she was skating on. If her mother ever found out that William Grant was in Glasgow, it'd be the death of her. If she found out that it was Morag who brought him here, she'd take her with her.

The plants at the front door all watered, she came down the hall and caught a glimpse of her mother getting out of the bath. Funny how people age differently. William Grant gave the impression of having slowed down with age. Her mother had speeded up. As though life had become a hassle and she wanted to get things done as quickly as possible. Make the tea, do the shopping, have a bath, go to sleep. There was a time back then, just after her little incident – as they called it – that Morag felt that, if she could, her mother would speed up life itself. Get it over and done with, out of the way. Like spring-cleaning.

She wasn't like that any more, thank goodness. More her old self these days. Still a bit agitated, jumpy, but out and about again, seeing for herself at home. Which left Morag feeling a bit nonessential. Still, she did what she could. She went into the kitchen to make them both their morning cup of tea; get the pencils and dictionaries out for the daily crossword. She dreaded her mother coming in. She'd know Morag was up to something. Wouldn't even need to hear her say anything – just the way she moved and sat would be enough. Her mother won't accuse her outright. She'll stay silent, talk about something else altogether, put on that disinterested face of hers, until Morag finally cracks and ends up shouting at her mother and telling her the truth. It's been like that ever since Morag was a kid.

She managed not to, though – blurt it all out. She was getting better at keeping things to herself. Both her counsellors – especially Pam, the nice one – had worked with her on this. She made her excuses and went home a little earlier than usual. Told herself on the way down the road how well she was doing with both William and her mother. Well, she was. She was being like her old self. A proper nurse. She was being patient. Sticking to the rules. She was doing just fine.

She'd let William Grant treat her to a few more meals like the one she'd had last night. He owed her that at least. No point in hacking him off, though. Couldn't be sure that his manners would stop him from calling in on Mother Dear unannounced for ever. She'd give him all the information she had, tell him, eventually, everything he wanted to know about George and Isobel and Grace, send him packing a happier man than he'd arrived. Once he'd heard the whole story, hopefully that'd be enough and he would-n't go making a nuisance of himself trying to see the old dear.

When she got home, there was a message for her on her answering service, which was a nice surprise. It was William, suggesting that instead of going for a meal tomorrow night would she mind, if she was free, going with him instead in the afternoon for a walk round Kelvingrove and the Botanic Gardens?

—I haven't been there for so long and, according to the forecast, tomorrow's going to be a dry day.

Fuck.

Actually, as it turned out, it wasn't too bad right enough. No sleet, not too much wind and what there was of it wasn't too snell. Didn't rain all day. A nondescript day in a nondescript city, thought Morag as William tried to enthuse about the parks. The reality was, the trees were drooping and weepy, the river mucky and full of crap, the people cold and bored. Windhoek must be a hell of a hole by comparison because William seemed genuinely impressed by the River Kelvin and the oaks and elms and the Kibble Palace with its collection of foreign trees and tropical fish. Kept going on about how you don't appreciate these places when you're young, and Morag was quite pleased that, compared to him, she *was* quite young really.

She worried, though, that William had forgotten all about her mother. He'd asked how she was when they first met at the gates of the Botanic Gardens, but then for the next two hours never mentioned her again. Nor Isobel. Nor Morag's father, nor made a single remark about the old days. All he was interested in was the trees and the buildings and the rivers and in which direction Bunnahabhain Road lay, and where was Maryhill. Perhaps the little she'd told him already had scared him off. Maybe he didn't want to know any more.

—I told you in my letter my mother was attacked, didn't I?

He stopped dead in his tracks.

—By whom? Was she badly hurt?

—Guy hardly touched her. She took it hard at the time, though.

They were back on the right track again, thank heaven. She felt more relaxed, glad to be talking about things that had happened yonks ago. Both Pam and the other counsellor agreed with Morag that she wasn't truly hung up about her past – despite it being such a shitty one. Pam's theory was that the reason Morag liked to talk about the past was because it was certain, unchangeable. Unlike the present or, worse, the future.

She was about to launch into a detailed description of what happened to her mother three years ago, when she noticed William was trembling in the cold. She's not a nurse for nothing, Morag. She notices little things, and Takes Action. She refused to tell him more until they were seated somewhere warm, led him by the arm to the café in the Gallery. Once she'd found them a table and'd bought a pot of hot tea and a plate of biscuits, she settled down to tell William everything she knew about the day her mother was mugged. Morag knew every detail, as if it'd happened to her personally. No wonder, the amount of times her mother's been over the same story. Time and time and time again.

In the first place, she shouldn't've been walking along South Policy Road that Friday afternoon at all. The obvious route home from the post office was via Kelso Street and Bunnahabhain Road, but her mother always avoided that area. She was collecting her pension a day late to fit in with a hospital appointment to have fluid drawn from her knees. Not a good idea. Her arthritic joints jar and scrape more on the days of the injection, and walking down to the post office, then to the shops and back, gave her gyp.

—Mother used to be very good at keeping herself busy. Always on the go. Sore joints or no.

William nodded, as though that was just how he would have expected her to have turned out.

—Voluntary work with the homeless, visiting elderly neighbours, that sort of thing. And of course, Arran House. Her children's home.

His face lit up, remembering.

—Her children's home. Of course! She got that off the ground.

—Half the west end ladies over fifty claim they were responsible for setting it up. The other half are still trying to pull it down.

—Good for Grace.

—Not that good for her, actually. He was from Arran House. The boy. The one that mugged her.

—Oh my God. She knew her attacker?

—Had Arran House written all over him. Rich, isn't it? Mum and Dad had always taught me not to be frightened of those kids but the little Fuckwits got her in the end.

Danger sign – swearing out loud. William didn't seem to notice. At least, he didn't react. Morag tried to calm herself. Talk more slowly.

—Anyway, Mother saw him coming at her, gripped her bag and tried to speed up. She knows what a kid like that's capable of.

—What did he do to her?

—Pushed her, that's all. But she fell against a railing behind her, put her neck out. Been giving her trouble ever since.

—Then what happened?

—That's all she can remember.

Morag took a sip of her tea, watched William stare out of the window. It occurred to her to leave it at that, not finish the story. That'd be the sensible thing to do. But then she thought, Why should I? William Grant of all people ought to share with her what happened next.

—*I* can remember something more, though.

She took another sip of tea, made him wait a little.

—I was on duty when she was brought into the hospital. She was still in shock. She opened her eyes and saw me and started talking a lot. She told me something she can't remember now, but I can. The boy had shouted something at her.

—What?

—He'd shouted, 'What are you doing here?'

William looked at her, puzzled, trying to figure out the meaning not just in the boy's words but in the importance Morag was giving to them. She looked coolly at the older man, the way she'd learnt to do when talking seriously to patients about their condition. Her old Truth Will Out look.

—My father used to ask my mother that same question. Poor old mum – she was confused, laid up in hospital after a fright like that. I'm used to it, though. Nurses get that a lot, you see. People talking to you, confused.

She was letting herself get upset again. Mustn't do that. Mustn't start thinking of things she shouldn't, saying things she'd regret.

—I don't understand.

—Probably, the boy never said any such thing to her. She was thinking of my father. 'What are you doing here?' he used to ask her. Over and over again. Just before he died. 'Why didn't you go away with him?' he asked.

William pushed his chair back and asked like a child if he could leave the table. He'd like to go home now.

Morag peeled the wrapper off a chocolate biscuit, sat up straight in her chair, mustered up one of her biggest, blondest smiles, and said, —Oh no. That'd be a shame. We're in the Art Gallery, after all. They say it's one of the best in Europe. We really ought to have a look round.

William looked at her as if she were mad. The idea must always have been at the back of his mind. He'd been far too polite to mention it, but Morag had never forgotten that in her first letter to him she said she'd seen folk ascending into the sky. Well, he can think what he likes. She's over that now. And he came here to find things out. If he didn't like what he was learning, he could lump it. As they left the café he glanced hungrily towards the exit, but dutifully followed her up the stairs. She whisked him through room after room, never stopping at any pictures. He paused, though, for a moment, at Courbet's *Poverty*. Looked at the spindly old beggar, as though he recognised himself. As they were about to go back outside into the cold she put her hand on his shoulder.

—I've come to a decision. Perhaps it's about time that you saw her after all. I can't really stop you, can I? Would you still like to?

William nodded gravely, and for a moment she thought he might cry. Might put his head on her shoulder and start blubbing like a wean. She was half terrified at the thought and half rather liked the idea. But he turned to start walking home, pale as a sheet. They headed for his hotel, hardly exchanging a word. As they got nearer Morag set up the meeting for Friday coming, when her mother would be out and about anyway. She could see he had a headache and couldn't get home quick enough. He was grimacing and putting his hand to his head a lot, dashing up the road, Morag lumbering behind as fast as she could, having a wee smile to herself every so often.

Morag didn't see him for the next three days. Nor did he telephone or leave any messages. She rang his hotel, just the once, to make sure he hadn't checked out and gone home. He hadn't, and she didn't leave any message for him.

Tuesday's the day she goes to the doctor, if she goes at all. She has a counsellor the doctor put her on to after she told him about her vision and her run-in with the McFarlane family. But she prefers Pam, another counsellor she picked herself from an ad in the window of the health shop on Dumbarton Road. Pam – a black girl, from London – doubles up in shiatsu, but Morag has never given that a go. Both shrinks, as she likes to call them, are once a month on a Wednesday. Neither of them this week, though.

Sometimes she met a few of her old nursing colleagues, to keep up with the goss, so that, once she got back to work, she wouldn't be absolutely in the dark about everything that was going on. This week she decided to give it a miss. Truth was, William had taken it out of her. All the worry of his arrival, and then the tension of meeting someone new, and *him* of all people. And all the talking and walking, and eating and remembering she'd done this week. She'd have to start all over again, come Friday, so for the next few days she took it easy. On Thursday, she'd go to the hospital, up to Personnel, have a just-passing chat with Mrs Kelly. Start putting in motion the wheels of her comeback.

She tried reading her biography. But it opened with complicated family tables of Scottish, English and French royal families. Then there was a quote from John Knox about all the world lamenting that the realm was left without a male to succeed the king. And then it went on about how cold it was in 1542, boats frozen into the harbour in Newcastle. She really wasn't in the mood for such drudgery. That was the thing about biographies, they only ever get written about people who were up to their oxters in dooh-dah, and that might be OK if you're not in it up to the oxters yourself.

Two afternoons in a row she sat, book on her lap, looking out the window. Over the church with its stubborn spire, towards more spires on the University and Art Gallery. She watched the people duck in and out of closes and shops, and the rain when it came on. She'd lived all her life in this part of the city. Funny, she thought, how you can live in a place all your life and there are still so many people you don't know from Adam. Where did all these strangers come from? Had she just grazed by all these folk for all these years? Walked out of shops just when they were walking in? Had they never had to go to the hospital when she was on duty in A&E? Where were these strange people's doctors, dentists, hairdressers if they weren't Morag's own doctor, dentist, hairdresser? That many folk, cheek by jowl, and not bumping into each other somewhere down the line.

The Fat Girl was right. We just don't see people. Some of them right in front of our noses, and we don't see them. She'd come up to Morag in the street, not that long after her mother's assault. Morag was on her way to the backshift at the hospital when the girl made a beeline for her. Made Morag nervous. She'd thought the girl was maybe going to beg and Morag wasn't lucky with beggars. Once, she'd been on the subway and was getting out at St Enoch's. There was a man standing there, holding out a cup. Trainers loosely covering bare feet like bandages, trousers held up at the waist with string. Morag searched in her purse while she waited for the escalator to take her up to him. She dropped a pound coin in his cup making hot coffee splash and spill, burning the man's hand. He shouted, Hoy! and Morag could just've died. So when the Fat Girl suddenly walked up to her, Morag didn't know what to expect.

—You're Miss Lapraik, in't you?

—No. I'm Mrs Simms. But I am Mrs Lapraik's daughter. Why?

—I'd talk direct to your old dear, only I wouldn't want to put the shits up her. I know who jumped her.

Morag couldn't speak.

—Tell her, would you, Canny didn't mean her any harm. She was just in the wrong place at the wrong time.

Morag tried to concentrate. The girl was volunteering crucial information. If Morag listened hard, she might be able to put the police on to the trail of the attacker. Having *him* put away would surely help her mother feel better about the whole thing.

—It was all my fault, really.

—And your name is?

—Margaret. You see, I slipped him a Mickey, without meaning to. There was this guy, Bubbles, who had it in for him. And through another friend he'd got a tab to me. Bubbles knew I'd either split the tab with Cannibal or give him it whole. It's a long story. I was told it was a chill pill. You know – Ativan?

Morag nodded. She did know.

—But it wasn't. It was acid. So when Canny saw your ma, he was out his box. Didn't know what he was doing.

—If he was really sorry, he'd come and speak to me or my mother in person.

—He's disappeared.

—Where to?

—Everyone says London when someone can't be found. But who knows – maybe he's gone back home.

—Where's that?

—Wish I knew.

The Fat Girl was so fat and scruffy she made Morag feel thin and groomed. Morag watched her waddle off, dragging her heels, head slumped low on her shoulders. You couldn't help but feel sorry for a girl like that. Morag set off in the direction of the police station. But then she realised that nothing the Fat Girl had said made any sense. A jumble of Cannibals and Bubbles and tabs and splitting. And it dawned on her that of course the girl wouldn't have been stupid enough to have used real names. Not even real nicknames. Cannibal and Bubbles didn't sound likely. Margaret even less so, for a girl who looked as unkempt and smelly as that.

Before she'd plodded off, the Fat Girl'd said she saw Morag and her mother all the time. If Morag kept her eyes peeled, she could find her too. That was about two years ago and Morag hadn't seen her since. Worrying, that. These crazy kids, you can't see them but they're watching you all the time, getting ready to pounce.

A city like this. Full of crazies – violent juveniles, weirdo old men, unhelpful library assistants, cheeky flower shop girls, snooty doctors, difficult patients, dying young women. It all made Morag want to swear. It made her want to do all sorts of unpleasant things, but swearing was the most practical. So she sat at her window and picked out individuals in the street. From this high up you could only tell sex and approximate age, few other details were visible. She picked out one figure at a time and called them Hag, Arsehole, Prat.

She went on like this for a full five minutes, screwing up her eyes, concentrating hard, grinding her teeth. She knew if she kept on doing it for long enough it'd reach a pitch, and she'd start to say the words out loud, hissing them at the window pane, the poor buggers down in the street oblivious to the fact that there was a sunny but competent forty-year-old staff nurse high above them calling them everything. After a few hisses, the need would subside and she'd be able to stop eventually, relieved.

She'd told one of the counsellors – the shiatsu one – about her thing for swearing. The counsellor supposed that, so long as no one was getting hurt and it made Morag feel better, then presumably there was no harm in it. Morag knew that wasn't true. It did her a lot of harm. She could feel somewhere inside of her getting more and more full of filth every time she swore into herself. Be better if she could swear *out* the way, directly *at* someone else for a change, instead of keeping all that crap inside her. Better out than in, as Mother used to say.

First swearing she ever heard was on trips to Arran House as a girl. Her mother used to take her, and sometimes her father went along too. They told her the Arran boys and girls couldn't help themselves, that they *had* to use these disgusting words. It was the way they were brought up. It was due to the Education System failing them. It was the way their parents spoke. Morag was to be sure not to copy them, to keep her ears closed, not to use those words herself. They were alien creatures those wiry, fully articulated kids with limbs like Plasticine that could bend in any direction. Morag was frightened of them, the way they clustered, spoke in strange tongues. But they provided Morag with her earliest collected words: keech, toley, wanker.

Then there was her father, when he was drunk, lying in his bed, shouting at her mother, filling the house with terrible words. Words that fluttered around the walls and windows like insects, jumped up out at her from the floor and under the bed like fleas, and Morag decided that one day she'd make sure she knew what those words meant. Slut. Hag. Cow.

Then, finally, there was Isobel. Miss Isobel Grant. Auntie Isobel. Of course, it was only towards the end that Isobel took up swearing, but when she did, she did it with a vengeance.

The police came one night to Isobel's big semi, sirens blaring, lights spinning, alerting all the neighbours. Morag ran down to Bunnahabhain with a schoolfriend, but arrived too late to see Nose-in-the-Air, Plenty-of-Mascara-but-Never-Wipes-her-Arse Miss Grant being led out the house, American-movie fashion, with a crook, who the papers later said was called Stanley Malone and was her boyfriend. After that, everyone also said that George Lapraik MP had been right all along. The Grant woman was a whoremonger. A procuress. A madame. Would you credit it? All these years running a brothel. In Bunnahabhain Road, for God's sake.

The police didn't keep her for long, though. She was taken away, brought back, taken away again, this time for longer, but brought back for good after a week or so. There was talk of a trial and prison and fines and all sorts of things, but Isobel probably just died too soon for due process to run its course. Still, she was a changed woman after the incident with the police. She still tried to dress posh, and strut in and out of shops expecting folk to be at her beck and call. But it never really worked after that. Within a few months, she was letting it all go. Not bothering dressing up. Going out to the shops in her slippers like a common charwoman. Muttering to herself. The only person who gave her house space was Morag's mother.

She used to come on Saturday mornings, when Mum would buy cakes and shortbread and fancy jams, special teas. Morag would try and be out, or in her room studying or listening to records when Isobel came by. Tim Buckley or Cohen or the like. She used to have a good collection, Morag – West Coast mainly, and the Velvets, angsty, druggy stuff. But her mother always insisted that she come in, even just for a minute, to say hello to Auntie Isobel. She could call her that now in the house, now that Dad had passed away.

Then she started going weird. Insisted that Morag's mother wear certain dresses, and have her hair in a certain way. Tied up at the back. Morag got angry at her mother doing whatever the old bag asked. Her mother said the poor woman was ill, and it was best to keep the peace. So though she had worn her hair short for years she still tried to pile it up to suit Isobel's request.

Isobel sat in her seat and muttered. At first Morag couldn't catch what she was saying. But then, eventually, she began learning new forms of abuse, as the half-mad old woman damned this and fucked that. Morag collected her first racial abuse: Darkie, Mick, Dago, Pape, Paki. And words that she'd later hear young folk in the street saying, and women locked up in asylums.

Couple of years after Isobel died, Morag started her nursing training. She had to do a stint in a women's psychiatric ward. Those women appalled her – their tragic histories, told at teabreak by nurses, like ghost stories round a campfire. Slow burning madnesses that start as charming childhood idiosyncrasies and end up leaving their victims in a living nightmare. Worse, when it was sudden. One woman, perfectly capable mother of three, until one morning, aged thirty-three, she suddenly lifted her porridge bowl and put it upside down on her head. Then she did the same to each of her astonished children. Soon enough she was in the locked ward, and used to re-enact the porridge ritual every morning – till they discovered that if they offered her cornflakes instead, she showed no desire to tip it over her own or anybody else's head.

Worse still, was the exhibitionism and aggression of the madwomen in her charge. They swore, undressed themselves in front of her, or better, in front of a man – doctor, visitor, whoever entered the ward. They'd grab at his crotch, or Morag's, or each other's, masturbated publicly on their beds or in the open toilets. And the foulest language imaginable. All things that, before their minds went haywire, would have outraged them. It terrified Morag that maybe, deep down inside her own mother or Isobel, herself for God's sake, there lay a woman like that. Perhaps a woman who witnessed apparitions on the streets of Glasgow was already halfway there.

Morag's mother was so embarrassed when Isobel swore, especially in *her* house and in the hearing of her daughter. She tried to get out of the Saturday morning teas, but could never bring herself to cancel them. Then came the morning, one of the last that Auntie Isobel was ever in their house, when Morag came in and instead of Isobel being in her normal chair, she was standing beside Morag's mother.

Isobel, more bedraggled that ever, was stroking her hair, like she were a child or something, touching her cheek, saying, – Grace, Grace, Grace Grace Grace.

The tears smudged Isobel's powdered cheek and Morag's mother just sat there, mortified.

—You're my sister, Grace. Always were. Always will be.

A little time later, Morag's mother managed to persuade Isobel to go to the doctor's. She went with her, and then to see some specialist in the hospital. She was with her again a few weeks later, when they told Isobel she was displaying early signs of Alzheimer's. However, she seemed to get better after that. Tidied herself up, and for a few weeks talked sense and went about her business, turning down offers of Saturday morning tea. Eventually,

though, the Alzheimer's did for her. One Sunday afternoon, she turned the gas on in the stove, had a loaf all
ready to cook on the middle shelf inside, but obviously had
forgotten to light the oven, or close the door. She'd sat
down to write something. A list of names, apparently. No
one could make head or tail of it. She fell asleep, and died
in the fumes.

When Morag, sixteen years old, was given the news,
she swore out loud for the first time in her life and her
mother scolded her for it. Thank Fuck, she'd said.

Anyway, Pam might be a dab hand at shiatsu, but she
knew bog all when it came to swearing. No doubt swear
words didn't stick to her the way they did to Isobel or
Morag. Didn't jump out at her in the street, or had been
flung at her since she was a kid. Morag knew their power
as she hissed down from her window over the street below.
Knew how they stayed inside you, like bile. She sat back in
her chair, exhausted from the tension of swearing inwardly.
She took a few deep breaths, felt herself relax, relieved,
then got up and put her book away, and went out to do
some shopping.

On Thursday night, she phoned home, told her mother
which café she'd be in, and at what time tomorrow
morning. If Mum fancied a coffee, she could join her. Her
mother said: That'd be very nice, dear. I might just do that.

Watching him make his way through the drizzle towards
her he looked frailer than he had three days ago. Of course,
he wasn't *actually* frailer. Just that, since last time they'd
met, Morag'd been doing some calculations. She'd passed a
sign when she was at the shops yesterday, on a pillar outside
Arran House that read, 'Est'd 1960'. She'd never really
noticed it before.

If William was on the scene when she was nearly four

years old, and he was in his mid-twenties when he left for Africa, then he must now only be in his mid-sixties. Just twenty odd years older than Morag. Twenty years. Twenty years ago she was going out with Michael. It was no time. No time at all. Yet twenty years ago, her mother wasn't that much older than she herself was now. And when she helped set up the home, she must only've been twenty-eight or so. Young. William wasn't even retiring age. Watching him now, he wasn't so much frail as fragile. He walked slowly for a man in his mid-sixties. So careful in his step, and dressed so perfectly it was as if he was trying to regulate himself out of existence.

They walked along the road a bit together, catching up on what each had done over the last couple of days, and she made it look as though they'd just stumbled across a convenient café just as her feet were beginning to hurt her. He'd be itching, of course, to know what the precise details of the meeting with her mother would be, but too polite to ask. All she'd told him was that she'd meet him this morning and, later on, they would meet up with Grace Lapraik.

As they entered the chip shop which had a café to one side of it, William enquired: —Didn't there used to be a café behind a bakery somewhere along there?

And he pointed with his fine leather-fingered glove up towards Dumbarton Road. Morag said she didn't think so. They ordered at the counter, sat down, and all the time he spoke, he glanced constantly out the window.

On Tuesday, he'd gone to the university and walked round the courtyards and cloisters, stuck his head into a few of the old lecture theatres he used to sit in, strolled past the students' union, and wandered around the adjoining streets and parkland. On Wednesday, which was a filthy day, he'd stayed close to the hotel, working.

—You have work to do while you're here?

—Not paid work. Mathematics is my hobby. I make up calculations for myself.

Morag laughed outright.

—What kind of calculations?

—Oh, it doesn't matter. Silly, really. I just try to make things add up.

—And do they? Add up?

—Never.

This time they both laughed.

Morag was alarmed to learn that on Thursday, the previous day, he'd gone flat-hunting.

—The hotel's too expensive for more than a week or so. A month's rent in a small flat will cost me considerably less than another week in the hotel.

—You're staying for a month?

—Probably not. But I doubt if I'll ever return to this part of the world again, so I might as well look around while I'm here. I've never been to a Scottish island before. I could do some fishing.

She picked up her cup, and turned away from him, looked out the window into the street. In this weather and through such a dirty window, it was like looking at a TV that's not picking up the station properly. Everything's shadowy and indistinct and so dull it looked like the old black-and-white days. Down towards the supermarket, a good deal earlier than she'd expected, she caught sight of her mother making her way up from the shops to the café. Morag tensed. Had to fight back a feeling of rising panic. Take deep breaths. Sit back and just let it happen. It'll be fascinating. Fascinating to see who recognises whom first.

Weird, though, watching her mother coming towards them. This little woman who had no notion that her lover of forty years ago was even in the same hemisphere, let alone sitting in the window of a café, right in front of her, like an Amsterdam whore. William had come six thousand miles to see one woman in particular but was oblivious to the fact that she was only a few yards away from him. One word to him from Morag, or a signal to her mother, and she could change both their lives. Do nothing, and she'd still change their lives – just, they wouldn't know it.

Morag felt as if she wasn't really there at all. It was as if she'd no option, no choice, but to sit there, impassive, an innocent bystander, incapable of affecting events. William was still talking and, dreamlike, she could see his lips move, hear the din of the café all around them, but not pick up a single sound from his lips. He had been glancing out into the street all morning. If he were to do so one more time within the next minute, he would see her. Morag's mum. Grace Lapraik.

How would they greet each other when she walked in? Who would say first, It's not really you, is it? Could it be? Well. My, my. Her mother would be angry with Morag, but would she show it here, in front of him? How disappointed would he be, travelling all this way to find someone so utterly ordinary? Would her mother smile, or cry, or laugh, or storm out, or what?

Morag looked at her through the murky television screen. A little lady, indistinguishable from all the other little ladies in a city jam-packed full of them. Pleasant enough face, but squat shoulders as though the city and the dark March skies were squashing her down. A shopping bag in either hand, a woollen hat on her head, wisps of hair wet hair from the drizzle. She spotted Morag, and walked straight towards the café window.

Came right up to the window and peered in. Morag turned to look at William. He was talking, and looking in the other direction, inwards towards the café. Then his head turned 180 degrees, right past Morag, and he looked directly out into the street. Morag held her breath as William and Grace looked right into each others' eyes, for the first time in nearly forty years.

Her mother nodded to William, then looked at Morag. William showed no signs of seeing anyone. He was still talking, his lips moving, and wasn't seeing what was in front of his nose.

Morag's mother mouthed to her: —I'll see you later.

She made a face and walked briskly off.

Morag burst out laughing and William smiled and said, —What's so funny?

—You'd have thought the least you could've done was recognise her!

Morag sat staring at her pizza, knowing too well she looked like a child throwing a tantrum. There was nothing she could do about it. There were tears welling in her eyes, a tenseness in her neck, and her face was set in a scowl that she couldn't change.

—In the name of heaven, Morag, I didn't even *see* the woman! It was a dull day, I wasn't looking, I don't know what she looks like. I didn't expect to see her outside a café window.

Yesterday, in the café, when she'd told him what had just happened – that he'd just looked right through the woman he'd waited nearly forty years and travelled thousands of miles to see – he'd got very annoyed and told her that that was a ridiculous thing to do. He'd stomped out the little café saying he could see now that she was mad enough to have visions of people rising up into the heavens. That hurt her, but what really worried her was that William, in his anger, would go straight to Grace and introduce himself. He hadn't, though, and last night he'd phoned to apologise and here they were the following evening sitting in a pizzeria.

—Not very romantic, though, is it? Not recognising her.

—You have a child's idea of human relations, Morag.

—What did you *think* she'd look like?

—I suppose I still see her as she was back then. I try to add a few wrinkles round the eyes, more grey hair, that sort of thing.

He said it's easy to follow the logical line of how someone changes when you see them constantly. You don't notice the day-to-day changes, but when you looked back at old photographs you could discern a logic, a natural course of events. The extra weight after the second child, then the laughter lines, then the jowls after that depressing time at work, and so on. But when you see someone for the first time in years, the change is unaccountable.

They didn't speak for a while, Morag struggling to shake off her mood. He was still annoyed and was punishing her with his silence. She used to do that to her mother when she was a child – stare at her and not utter a word. Of course, Mother was getting her own back these days. That was her technique – say nothing and wait until Morag cracks. Works a treat every time. That wasn't what William was up to, though. He was just being the strict teacher, the disappointed father. They gave up on their pizzas, and he asked for the bill without bothering to see if she wanted sweet or coffee.

While he was waiting for the waiter to return, he asked, as though the thought had just crossed his mind: —Did *she* recognise *me*?

Morag shook her head.

—You did tell her that she saw me?

She nodded and William sighed, signed the bill and they got ready to leave.

She had told her mother no such thing, of course. She'd

told her the man she was with in the café was a friend. Her mother had hoped that it might be a doctor from the hospital and Morag had said: Yes, yes it was. So, was there a chance of her getting her old job back soon, then? Yes to that too. Morag had smiled and said: Why didn't you come in, join us? And her mother said, No, she didn't want to spoil Morag's chances. Morag smiled but she suspected that, really, her mother knew something was afoot. Was on to her.

The waiter brought William his credit card back. William helped her on with her coat and gave her a little smile – the first one of the evening. He had forgiven her, presumably. She tried to smile back, but her face muscles weren't responding yet. She was still feeling guilty. Partly about what she had done in the café yesterday, partly out of worry that she was pushing William Grant's good nature too far.

Following him out of the restaurant she thought she might lose him, the way she'd lost Michael and her father. His patience would run out, like everyone's always did. Only a week ago she'd been in a state about his coming over here. Now she didn't want him to leave. Once he left, life would be back to normal. She'd be the same old Morag, and nothing would have changed, nothing would have happened. Her world would be an Africaless place again. A place where the past was lost, made wordless. A place without a future. It was doing her good, having William around. Taking her out of herself.

Outside it was bitterly cold but not raining. William brightened a little.

—I miss this kind of weather. What d'you say we walk the whole way home?

—Are you kidding?

She'd catch her death. She wouldn't be able to make it.

She hadn't walked further than a couple of hundred yards for donkey's years.

—Pity, he said, and they turned and set off towards the taxi rank at Central Station. When they got there, there was a queue miles long.

—I really think we should start walking. We'll freeze standing around in this temperature.

She had no choice but to follow him, and they began marching westwards.

—When will you go home?

—Soon.

—What about your flat?

—I'll move in on Monday. Make use of it for a few days. It'll take me into next week to organise my travel.

—You'll go and see Grace. Won't you?

—No. *This* time I want to be properly introduced. Or not at all. So it's up to you, my dear.

He grimaced, changed the subject, walked on.

—Thought I might stop off a couple of times on the journey home. Paris. Then Lagos maybe. I can't see me ever leaving home again, might as well make the most of it. I'll hire a car tomorrow, take a couple of days in the country here.

The mention of such exotic places made Morag feel more miserable than ever. She'd been abroad before, of course. With a bunch of nurses, to Spain, and Italy, Greece. And once she took her mother on a weekend break to Amsterdam, to try and cheer her up after her incident. She'd travelled a fair bit all right, and wasn't overly romantic about foreign places. She'd been harassed in Italy, had her passport stolen in Spain, been cheated in restaurants in Holland. It's just that those places of William's — Paris, Casablanca, Windhoek — were *other* places. Not here. Even up north, or the islands he wanted to visit, were somewhere else. Everyone seemed to have travelled somewhere in their lives. She'd hardly moved spitting distance from where she was born. William had moved halfway across the world. Her mother had only moved from Gourock, but that was a big change in its way too. Michael, reportedly, had a house in some fancy part of London. Paris had sailed to the moon, got tangled up in the clouds. But Morag was landlocked, tightly roped and ballasted down by the double weight of her body and her past.

She was surprised to see how quickly they'd got to Dumbarton Road, despite the temperature being freezing. Lost in her bad temper, and numbed by the cold, they'd got to the Kelvin Hall before she knew it. They walked on, past the Cross, then William stopped suddenly, looked around, at both sides of the road, then up at the sky. She half expected him to sniff the air.

—What?

—It was here. The café. Tearoom. The place I used to meet your mother in. Now that I see it without cars.

Morag looked around.

—There's no café here.

—That Chinese restaurant. Or the place next door, the newsagent's. But definitely on this block. That side. That was the last place I ever saw her.

William stood staring at the doorways and windows of the shops on the other side of the deserted road. Morag waited, used to the cold now and past caring. His voice was thin and sharp in the night air and, being in this spot, he no longer cared about covering up a forty-year-old illicit relationship.

—We ordered tea and scones like we always did. We both knew I was leaving, but still we spoke about George and his career, and politics. And about you. Always about you.

He turned to look at her, and fell silent for a moment, as though he was making the connection for the first time between that child nearly forty years ago and the big, blonde woman walking a step or two behind him.

—You were the first topic of conversation, and when we parted, the last. It used to annoy me. I knew everything about you – your favourite books, your best frock, what you'd eat, what you wouldn't.

Morag looked at him for a moment, and gave a little laugh. She knew that must be true. Could hear her mother telling him that sort of stuff. Talking about her. She still did, to an extent. Was proud of her daughter being a staff nurse. Was forever privately trying to make up for the bad years, and Morag would respond angrily, reminding her just what it was that led to her father's drinking, his death, who was the whore, why they were in the situation they are now.

—Finally, I worked up the courage to ask her if I should do as George wanted me to do.

William was half in shadow, some of the streetlights out as usual. Some nights this city looks like a shanty town. You couldn't see his grey, receding hair, and Morag tried to imagine what he must have looked like at twenty-four. What her mother must've been like.

—What *did* he want you to do?

—To leave, of course.

—And what did she say?

—She said yes. Thought it was probably the right thing to do.

William said he tried for an hour to get her to tell him to stay, and then another half-hour persuading her to come with him. Morag laughed.

—You mean, I could have grown up in Namibia? I could've been African?

—I doubt it. It was just a way of keeping her there with

me for a while longer. There was no possibility of me staying, or her leaving. Eventually I gave up. I asked if it'd be all right if I left the tearoom before her.

His voice was quiet, and he'd begun walking very slowly along again. Glanced back at the Chinese restaurant. Morag walked along right next to him, almost having to bend towards him to hear the words.

—I looked in through the window at her. She didn't look up. She seemed resigned. Relieved, almost. Then I went to the hospital to say goodbye to my mother. I banked the cheque your father'd given me, into the family account. Never imagined it would end up causing so much trouble.

They came to the street his hotel was in, and they both stopped at the corner.

—At home I saw Isobel. She sat on her bed with a large ledger in front of her. Columns of names in it. Women's on one side of the page, men's on the other. Names I knew, from around here. I wonder how many families there are now, thanks to Isobel. There was a photograph of an uncle of ours lying upside down on her dressing table, broken glass all around it. I said I was leaving. That I'd just paid a cheque into the family account. That I'd send more money from Africa soon. She said she didn't want my money. Later, I sent her cheques. But they were never cashed.

They walked in silence to his hotel door and William stopped at the bottom of the steps. He asked Morag to come inside while he ordered a taxi for her. But she said she wanted to go home, straight away.

—You know what the last thing I ever said to my sister was? That she would never make anyone happy.

He coughed and looked around, tried to look cheerfully at her.

—Come on in, please. I'll order you a taxi.

—No thanks. I'm used to walking now. Might as well go the whole hog.

—If you insist.

—What was the last thing you and my mother ever said to each other?

—Before I got up to leave the teashop, she touched the back of my hand.

He looked at the back of his hand now, red and raw with cold and age, as if her touch had branded him for life.

—Repeated an old joke we had between us.

—Which was?

He looked boyish, embarrassed.

—How we made angels and devils sing together.

He laughed, shook his head.

—Ridiculous, don't you think?

Morag walked home alone. Unaware of her tired legs and the cold. Tonight, she didn't feel angry and she didn't feel happy. She wasn't swearing at anyone, and she didn't want to go home and swear at herself. She tried to think of her mother, imagine her as a woman who could say such a thing. She felt numb and, although she was walking, she felt suspended somehow, and rather liked the sensation.

Next morning, Morag went to church. She wasn't a believer, she just needed time and space to consider what to do next.

Whenever she went into a church she always thought of Helen – a patient of hers during her stint in the psychiatric wards. Morag used to take her and a few others to the Sunday service, as much to get out of the ward as anything. Poor woman's condition included some form of catatonia, and the senior nurses in the mental ward warned Morag that if she began to move at all, if she unfroze herself, Morag was to get her back to the ward, quickstyle. You just didn't know what Helen would do, when she let herself go.

And one morning, she moved, right enough. Morag was a rookie nurse at the time, began to panic. Helen slowly uncurled herself in her chair, arms and fingers lifting and turning like a ballet dancer's. Morag managed to get her out of the church and back up to the hospital before any real damage was done.

But, leaving the church, Helen pointed up at the little minister in his pulpit and declared to the entire congregation, in a booming voice: —See that man? He's hung like a stallion.

Helen *knew*, she screamed. Had seen it. Wanted to see it again. She yelled at the poor clergyman who stood up there, bug-eyed, not daring to utter a sound, the whole congregation staring at the madwoman as she bawled her head off about how she wanted the vicar to do to her again all the things he'd done to her last night. Later, back at the ward, it was a good laugh. At the time it was excruciating.

In this church, this morning, Morag realised that she had to make a break. Something had to give. She couldn't go on this way. She would have to tell her mother that William was here and let the two of them meet, if they wanted. Not for her mother's sake, and certainly not for William Grant's. For her own. She had to make changes in her life. Get her job back. Or something. Take action.

On the Monday, late snows falling, she went to see the Personnel Officer at the hospital. Not officially, but just to bump into her accidentally-on-purpose in the staff canteen. Theoretically, Morag shouldn't've been there at all when she was off on the sick, but Mrs Kelly didn't mention the fact. They had a cup of tea together and Morag told her how much better she was feeling these days, and that she was dying to get back to work. Mrs Kelly smiled and said that that would be wonderful, all Morag had to do was bring a letter from her doctor and then they'd have a chat, the pair of them, see what they could do. Morag gave her a big, bright smile and went back outside.

Fuckwit. Kelly had no intention of letting her back. You could tell, just by the way she was talking to her. Well, who cares what Kelly says, Morag'll just go over her head, if necessary. She walked down the drive to the hospital gate, out on to Dumbarton Road, and headed back home. She tried like mad not to cry. She'd just been telling Mrs Kelly how she was over her bad patch and here she was walking along and couldn't get Paris out of her mind.

Making that journey, in her head at least, Paris had dreamt it was a sunny morning. Today was dark and dank. A covering of grey slush had slowed the city down. There was less traffic than usual and the rooftops from the university to the hospital and beyond, up the hill, were shrouded. Parked cars frozen crisp, grubby slush around their tyres. How could Paris have seen this place as so bright and sunny? It was last March she died, and the weather then had been even worse. Wouldn't it be wonderful if Morag could see the city like that? The way Paris had seen it.

She kept glancing back, hoping for a bus, but none came. She walked all the way along the semideserted main street, then up into Policy Road. Not her usual route – the hill normally being too much for her bulk. She wheezed and strained, and the trees drooped and seeped around her. Early buds wilted in the damp, all growth, like most of the city's transport, temporarily suspended. Then the sleet turned to cold rain – the kind of drizzle you feel before you can see, as though it's not falling from the sky but that the city itself is dissolving around you in the sodden air. Morag struggled her way up the hill, out of breath, sweating inside her warm coat. She thought of Paris, could imagine her skipping up the hill, so light on her feet, so hopeful, waving to her family at the top of the hill, the family poor Paris so firmly believed had never let her down.

Morag mustn't let herself get angry about the McFarlanes. She'd been making progress, didn't want to set herself back. They lived just over the hill there at 17 Dudhope Road. She could go there right now, tell them all over again what she thought of them. It was obvious that Kelly was never going to let her back into the ward, so what had she to lose? She tried to concentrate on what the counsellors – both of them – agreed. It wasn't the McFarlanes' fault. The night Paris's condition deteriorated badly, the doctors'd said it wasn't critical enough to contact the family. So Morag stayed with her, and tried to do what none of them – her mother or father or boyfriend or brother – ever had the guts to do.

That daft lassie really believed her cancer had been stopped dead in its tracks. Totally convinced she was getting out because the sickness had gone, once and for all. She had, of course, been informed of the true situation by her consultant. But it hadn't registered. Morag spent that long night trying to get through to her, trying to tell her the truth. But Paris just kept on smiling at her and talking about showers and combing her hair, and in French, and about her oh-so-wonderful family. Even after Morag took it upon herself to phone them in the middle of the night, they were still more than an hour getting to the ward. They only lived fifteen minutes away, for crying out loud. And when they got there, Paris smiled so happily at them. Morag had to slip away, let them play Happy Families.

She would have left it like that if it hadn't been for the glimpse she got of Paris, weeks later, rising up into the sky. She felt as if it was some kind of message and she had to do something about it. So she wrote the letter to William

Grant and the next day marched right into 17 Dudhope Road and gave that useless family a piece of her mind. All hell was let loose, and before long Morag was suspended from her job. Well, nothing to stop her from marching round there again now and giving the McFarlane Fuckwits a proper what for. Nothing to lose.

But she mustn't. She mustn't. She'd been doing so well. And William was here now. Things were about to change. She knew that now. The way ahead beginning to form in her mind. At the top of the hill, she turned and headed for her mother's house. She'd decided on Sunday morning that it was up to her to make things happen. And now that she knew exactly what it was she had to do, there was no time to lose in doing it.

On Tuesday morning she was very busy indeed. She got up early and popped in first to an estate agent's off the Byres Road to put her flat on the market, then into the alternative medicine clinic where she managed to change her usual Wednesday session with Pam to today, then into the library to hand in her book. She didn't bother to get a new one out or speak to the boring little library man, but spent a little time in the health and medicine section doing some research. Next, she phoned William from a call box. He wasn't in, but she left a message saying she would call by his new flat for him at eight tonight. She went for a coffee to fill in the time before seeing Pam, her counsellor.

—I don't want my old job back. Ever.

—Bit extreme, isn't it?

—I did the job for twenty years and was very good at it. Now they don't want me back, and I don't want to go back.

—*Never* go back to nursing? After all your training and with all your experience – that's quite a jump.

—I didn't say I would never go back to *nursing*. I don't want my old job back, that's all.

—It may be every bit as hard to get a new job as your old one back again.

—Well if you write me a letter saying that I'm of sound mind, in your opinion, and that I merely had a bit of a breakdown and am over it now, then that'd help, wouldn't it? If I got one from the doctor, and the counsellor the doctor put me on to, then that'd help too. Mrs Kelly I'm pretty sure *has* to give me a reference.

Pam argued that her written opinion may not carry much weight, but in the end she wrote out a little personal letter saying that she had treated Morag Simms for a mild nervous disorder, that the patient had responded well and that, in her opinion, Morag was fully recovered and there was no reason to expect that she'd necessarily suffer another breakdown.

Morag thanked her, got ready to go and said: —I may miss the next few sessions. I'm going away for a while.

—Anywhere nice?

—Don't know yet.

—We'll pick up from where we left off when you get back.

Morag passed people in the street she knew, but was too busy to stop and chat with them. She gave them all a quick smile and a Hi, and carried on with her list of Things to Do.

She went to the hospital, left a letter for Mrs Kelly, asking for a reference for her twenty years' work as a nurse in the Western Infirmary. Told her she was thinking of applying for jobs elsewhere in the profession. She popped along to Level 6, sought out Miranda, a doctor she used to be very friendly with. They both went to the canteen and Miranda happily wrote her a letter of recommendation, and a prescription that Morag wanted. She then went to her doctor's, left another note asking for a letter giving her the all-clear and requesting an appointment in the next week or so.

She treated herself to a light lunch in a little restaurant that she and Michael used to go to. At least, it was the same place, but quite a different establishment now. In the old days it was an Indian restaurant. Now it was French. While she ate her deep-fried courgettes, then her veal with a glass of white wine, she wrote to a few friends and ex-colleagues saying she was fine but she might not be around for the next few weeks as she was planning some holibags for herself. She'd send them all a postcard and get in touch just as soon as she got back.

She returned home – via the post office, the chemist's and Woolworths – late afternoon. She put on a regular daily wash, then went through her wardrobe and dressing table and looked out a selection of underwear, dresses, tops, skirts and either washed them too, or ironed them. The bottom of the wardrobe's the place she keeps her shoes, but she hasn't been in there for a year now, making do with an old flat-heeled pair, a pair of boots and slippers. She couldn't face her other shoes. Each time she went to look through them, the memory of Paris McFarlane, asking her to put a pair of shoes on her feet, threatened to flood her mind.

The pathetic girl'd been lying there, mumbling, talking about having a shower, then she'd looked directly at Morag and said: —My shoes?

She kept on and on asking for shoes, until finally Morag caved in. She found, in the bedside cabinet, an old pair of brown shoes that the girl had used for trips out across the hospital yard. Put them on her skinny, bony feet as she lay there in her bed. Paris was so happy once she had them on, started mumbling again about walking along Dumbarton

Road, or some place in France, while Morag sat by her side, shaking.

Ever since, she'd had a thing about shoes. Today, though, she simply had to look out a few decent pairs. So she began opening up the bags and boxes with her best footwear in them and let the memory of Paris rush over her. Afterwards, she had to go and have a bath, and then wash her face a couple of times more, splash her eyes. But she'd managed to get the shoes out. That was the main thing.

She got dressed and went out to meet William.

—But you flew in the night you arrived. You said so on the phone.

She'd been about to sit down after having seen round William's new flat – small, neat, characterless, looking the wrong way over Great Western Road, away from the parkland and the city centre. She stood sullenly in the middle of the little living room, glaring at him accusingly.

—Only from Liverpool, I'm afraid.

—I just assumed . . .

William explained to a crestfallen Morag that he'd returned to Scotland the same way he'd left, forty years ago. Of course, they didn't have cellular container ships way back then – his cabin on the return journey had all mod cons, but the vessel was nowhere near as elegant as he remembered the steamer he'd gone out in. Forty years ago, the ship he'd sailed in had carried a fantastical collection of livestock, grain, machinery parts, tweed, whisky, canned fish, sewing machines and gadgets from Singer in Clydebank. A little floating Scotland, he remembered thinking. On the way back the same boat would've carried minerals and ores, uranium, wood, artefacts, other kinds of dried and canned fish, marble, even gems and diamonds. A mini South-West Africa.

Morag tried to listen, but all this talk of ships was confusing her. She'd had it all clear in her mind how she'd make her escape. This was a major stumbling block. Trust William to go and throw a spanner in the works, travel halfway across the world in a flaming container ship, in this day and age. As he talked on, comparing his first voyage with his latest, she tried to think her way through the problem. She used to be good at that. That was why she was a promoted nurse. She was good at Finding a Solution, Getting Things Done, no matter what the snag.

The ship he'd disembarked from two weeks ago had got him here much quicker, even though it must've been about ten times the size. Carried nothing but grain and granite. Could manage far greater distances without stopping. It'd set out from Walvis Bay with stops scheduled for Lagos and Freetown, but both were declared too dodgy, so they stopped off for a full day and night in Lomé, instead. Then Dar el Beida, which used to be Casablanca, and William found the crossroads where his traffic policeman had been, and was disappointed to find that there were lights there now. They came up into mainland Britain via the Mersey instead of the Clyde.

—Even if I *had* flown all the way, Morag, it isn't possible just to hand someone over the ticket. They're untransferable.

—I thought we could have gone to the travel agent, or the airline or somewhere. You could have cancelled your ticket and I could have bought the freed-up seat.

—I doubt that would have worked.

Morag excused herself and went to the loo. She locked the door and sat on the toilet seat, swallowed back threatening tears. She wanted to swear out loud but managed to swallow all that too. She'd find out how much the journey was. Pay for it by herself, if she could. It wasn't the money that bothered her. But if she was simply going to buy her own ticket – well, she could have done that any old time. It wouldn't feel so much like seizing a unique opportunity. She sat in there for an age, trying like mad to think. By the time she unlocked the door and stepped, smiling, into the little living room, she'd got the answer.

—I'll travel by container ship too! An adventure to start my adventure! You can arrange that, can't you, William?

She looked eagerly at William, proud of her ability to work through a problem and come up with a solution. But William just stared at her, as if she were speaking in a foreign language he'd never come across. For the next half-hour she tried to persuade him, while he showed her how ludicrous her suggestion was. For one thing, he said, it was a very long, uncomfortable, dangerous journey.

—You did it. At twenty-four. Without ever having travelled before. And again as a man approaching retirement age. Can't be that bad.

Patiently, he explained how you can't just swap tickets for a container ship. William Grant, accountant, advisor to the Namibian Government, was their guest. Not Morag Simms, Glasgow nurse. It's not normal to have passengers who are not directly concerned with the cargo.

—You're such a big noise in your country. If you can arrange it for yourself, then you can arrange it for me.

How would William himself get back home?

—Take the next boat. If there's room on the same ship, then we'll travel together. Or fly home. If you can afford a flat at the drop of a hat, and The Devon for a week, you're well enough off to buy a plane ticket. I'll pay you back, once I've earned some money.

He asked how she intended to earn money. Where would she stay in Namibia? Or, if it was her intention to get off somewhere before Namibia, then where? What would she do?

He explained the complexities of visas and work permits, the near impossibility of finding desirable employment in Africa these days. He told her about the vaccinations she'd need and that some had to be got months ahead of travelling. He described the political instability of much of the continent, from Algeria south to Jo'burg. Mentioned the gangsters in Lagos, listed insurrections and civil upheavals from Sierra Leone to Angola and in the north of Namibia itself. He said Africa has long been a perilous destination for a lone woman traveller, and was even more so these days. But Morag had the whole thing worked out in her head.

—I've read up on what you need, vaccination-wise, in the library. I've been to the chemist's and bought the ones I can administer myself. I've got my malaria pills and I've got an appointment with my doctor later in the week, so all that'll be cleared up no bother. As for work permits, that'll be easier done in the country, no? I'll have a month's grace to see to that. I kind of hoped that either you or your daughter or your son would've had some influence with the hospitals in your country.

William argued that this was tantamount to corruption and of course neither Libertina nor Alphonse would help in any way. Morag said, sure they would. Especially after they'd met her. Once they saw how eager she was to work, and what a Sunny but Efficient kind of person she was. Morag wasn't bothered where she worked, what kind of hospital or in what post. Once she had a foot in the door, she'd work her way up. That's what she'd always done. They could post her to a hospital in the capital, or in one of the other towns, or even in the bush, or by the coast.

—Up north would be interesting. The Caprivi Strip.

—There's a virtual war going on up there!

—All the more need for nurses.

Morag got angry at him. He had no idea how experienced she was. Accident & Emergency on Friday nights in a town like Glasgow looks pretty much like a war zone. She'd seen things he'd never see. Heard things he wouldn't believe. She'd always been up to the job, no matter how messy, how alien, how brutal or dangerous to herself. She's got fifteen years more experience of life under her belt than he had when he went abroad.

—Ah but you see, that's the problem, isn't it? Isn't it a bit late to be thinking of doing such a thing?

—Of course not.

—What about your mother? And how do I explain *you*, Morag? Over there. In Namibia. You must understand, no one there knows of Grace's, let alone your, existence.

Morag laughed outright. William's little penitent sinner's face was hilarious.

—What is there to explain, William? You're making it sound like I'm your lovechild. I'm a friend of the family, who needs a break. That's all there is to it.

Then, with a smile, she added that perhaps one day, when she was settled and had a job and maybe even a place of her own to live, then Grace could come over and visit.

—Is that a threat?

To which Morag laughed even louder and said: Of course not. What on earth's threatening about it?

William sighed and looked up at the ceiling.

—I should never have come, he said, shaking his head.

She could feel his resistance ebb away. It was a lovely feeling. In the wards Morag was always able to talk patients – and sometimes even doctors – round. She had the knack of wearing them down, without pissing them off. It all had to do with persistence, tact and having bags full of energy.

William put on his spectacles and looked at her sternly over the rims. This was his last, gallant attempt. She knew the look.

—Aren't you supposed to be ill?

Morag gaily told him all about the letters of recommendation, the all-clears and references she'd organised. If she had a letter of introduction from him too, that'd be a help.

—Leaving's what'll cure me. I've decided, William. I'm going to do what you would have done. Fly to Liverpool, sail from there. I'll buy my own airline ticket. It's about time I had an adventure. Everyone I know's had an adventure, except me.

—You're asking a lot of me, Morag, and I'm not sure all – or any – of this is possible. What if I say no?

She leant towards him and spoke in her best staff nurse voice.

—You'll have let me down. And I think you owe me. It'd be honourable of you to help me out now.

She sat back comfortably in her chair and spoke again in a bright, loud voice.

—Also, there's Mum. She'll run a mile if you contact her direct. I'll do my go-between bit, for you and her, if you do the same for me – be the go-between between my old life and my new one.

—That's bribery, Morag.

—No it isn't. It's a deal. You know all about deals.

She got up, picked up her coat and headed for the door.

—It all adds up perfectly, William.

Morag's mother stared into space, glancing every now and then at Morag, her lips moving as if she were about to say something, then thinking better of it. Morag waited. She had no idea what was going on inside her mother's head, or what she might finally do, once the news had sunk in. She looked a bit lost and helpless, shaken. The way she'd looked in the days after her incident.

Morag liked those days. Those few weeks when her mother was almost wholly dependent on her. When she'd got out of hospital she'd stopped going out of the house at all and Morag went for all her shopping, rang or dropped notes to her friends every now and then, to keep them all at bay, looked after her. Morag had loved all that. Then coming home and making the old girl her tea, helping her with her bath, washing her hair, looking after the house. Made Morag feel like a good person. A professional Good Person, doing her bit back home. Putting to good use all those years of Training and Experience. And during that special time, her mother had talked a lot, which was out of character. That was when Morag found out so much more about both her own past and her mother's. She heard all about Gourock and the Houses of Parliament and the Truth About Isobel. If that bloody woman, her mother used to say, hadn't caught Alzheimer's I swear to God I'd have wrung her neck with my own two hands.

But within a few weeks, she was on the mend. Morag'd told her to take her time, there's no rush, but the daft old biddy'd insisted on getting back on her own two feet again. She began to accompany Morag out to the shops, take a bath by herself, and after a while even lock the door, which Morag thought was a very bad idea. She began to meet up with her old friends again and read the papers, books, listen to the radio. Soon enough she had no qualms about even walking around on her own with her handbag and purse. Of course, Morag kept right on worrying – who wouldn't? – but there was nothing she could do. Anyway, they'd moved her at work, put her in charge in one of the most difficult wards – terminal and long-term cancers – so she had to concentrate on that. Truth was that although she'd given William all that bunkum about her mother being a bag of nerves and sickly, her old dear had made a full and complete recovery. It took Morag herself a little longer to get over all the upset.

She hadn't lied about the impact William Grant's reappearance would have on her mother, though. Look at the state of the poor old dear now. Doesn't know where to look or what to say. Morag had told her as gently and as kindly as she could. Then waited for the reaction.

She didn't know what to expect – her mother to break down, sobbing. Or shout and bawl and Morag having to console her. Or start throwing things around, in which case Morag would simply have to keep her cool and let her get it out of her system and not scream back at her like she used to. Like the old days.

At last her mother gave a little cough, straightened up in her chair and asked Morag warily:

—I didn't recognise him?

Morag shook her head.

—And he didn't recognise me?

Her mother laughed out loud.

—Fancy that.

—Would you like to see him?

Her mother nodded. Not a nod from which much could be deduced, admittedly. A minimal nod, head slightly cocked, suggesting mild curiosity. But there was a tautness around her mother's mouth that indicated either her curiosity was much greater than she was letting on, or else perhaps that the whole idea was quite obnoxious to her.

—I'll ask him to collect me from my flat. He can buzz up on the intercom. We'll be upstairs at the window. If you feel like it, you can come down with me. If not, at least you'll have seen him, and he still won't know where you yourself live.

—Couldn't he find that out if he really wanted to?

—William likes to do things correctly. He'd want any meeting sanctioned, properly organised. Above board.

—That sounds like him.

—If he was going to barge in he'd have done it before now. I think he'd wait for ever, to do things the right way.

Then her mother leant over, touched her arm.

—Why is this so important to you, darling?

—Are you serious? said Morag, looking at her mother, incredulous. Jesus, this was about *her* – Grace Lapraik – not Morag. She waited for the old anger, the perennial need to scream at her mother to rise up inside her. It didn't really. It was there, but controllable.

—You must have been very upset when you wrote to him.

For Chrissakes, who was the nurse here? *Morag* was supposed to be helping *Mother* through some bad news, face up to the past! She'd expected her to shout, throw accusations, whatever. Not turn the tables.

—After that girl died. You haven't mentioned her in a while.

—It's got nothing to do with her!

A few dirty words fluttered around in her mind, but they died away quickly enough after a deep breath and her mother'd stopped asking questions. In silence, she cling-filmed the sandwiches neither of them had eaten, put some in her bag to take to her own flat, washed the cups, agreed the details with her mother about the sighting of William, and made her way home.

When she got in, she did a tour of the flat, doing little odd jobs as she went along. Dabbing paint on chipped woodwork, tightening the screws on a shelf that'd been sagging for months, looking out cardboard boxes and beginning to put away items which she knew she wouldn't need. Tomorrow, she'd have to find out about storage. She'd leave most of her stuff here until she settled elsewhere, then send for it.

She'd thought she might have been more uptight after the conversation with her mother. In fact, she'd been on a rather even keel for most of the afternoon and evening. But, after she'd had her bath and got ready for bed, sitting having a cup of tea in front of the telly, she began to get palpitations. It worried her for a moment. She'd experienced palpitations for the first time in her life that night with the McFarlane girl, then again before she went to see Paris's family. After that she'd begun to get full-blown panic attacks. Dizziness, blackouts, the lot. The symptoms had gone away over the last few months, but she worried this might be some kind of a setback. Then she reckoned it was all just down to the big change she was making, no point in worrying about it. She went to bed early and fell asleep at once.

She woke up early and leapt straight into action. She phoned her lawyer and got him to deal with the sale of her flat while she was away. She organised the removal and storage of her furniture. Phoned the bank, cancelled orders for papers and magazines, extended her credit card limit to £2,500. Then she made some sandwiches and a pot of tea and when her mother arrived at two o'clock they went into the kitchen and chatted like two old friends over lunch. Catching up, without ever mentioning the old days. At twenty minutes to three she led her mother through to the living room, taking her arm, as if she were crippled or very elderly.

Morag's mum was neither of these things. Probably,

she was as sprightly as Morag herself. Sprightlier, given Morag's weight problem, which was a genetic thing, nothing to do with her upbringing. Morag's father was pretty hefty towards the end. Still, her mother let herself be led into the room anyway, without saying anything.

—What time's he coming past for you, dear?

—Quarter-to.

Her mother looked at her watch and said:

—He's never late.

Morag had seen photographs of her mother around the time that William was on the scene. She hadn't aged that much in the last forty years, really. Maybe that was why William hadn't recognised her. She'd looked older than her years when he first met her, so probably he assumed that she'd kept right on ageing rapidly. But, in fact, she was wearing pretty well for a woman in her sixties. People often said she could be nigh on ten years younger, by the look of her. She ate well and healthily, especially after Dad had died, and walked a lot. Walked everywhere. That day in the café, William'd been on the lookout for an old woman. But Grace, at sixty-six, was slim, with thick white bushy hair, and if not exactly young-looking in her features, she was energetic, still a little nervous, and darted around like a woman half her age.

She did what she always did in Morag's flat, scouted around fixing antimacassars and straightening photographs and ornaments and saying what a lovely flat it was. So bright. Even on a wishy-washy day like today. Then they sat on the chairs that Morag had arranged in the small bay window. Settled down as if the window were a big screen and they were about to watch a film, or the Queen's Speech. Morag proudly pointed out all the things that could be seen from that window, though her mother had looked out it a million times before. The river. The University and its spire. Elegant Park Circus. Kelvin Hall. The SECC and the new Armadillo building. Her mother got up on her tiptoes to look north-west up the river. Said she used to hate the old Fascist-looking shipyard buildings, reminding Morag of what William had said about her being politically minded once. Beyond them lay Greenock and Gourock, where Grace and George's distant past lay. And then they moved over and looked out the other bay, upriver, eastwards towards the domes and angels and spires and crosses of the city centre.

—Is that him?

Her mother had seen William before Morag had. It was him all right. The great William Grant. Local boy made good. From up here you couldn't make out the quality of his coat, or catch the waft of cologne in his hair, or detect the careful rhythm of his gait. All you could see was an older man with a black coat, the wind blowing his thinning hair up into the air a little, a smudge of red on his lapel from the flower he had taken to wearing in the last few days. He was looking around for number 52. There was nothing unusual in the house numbering in this street, 52 being precisely where you'd expect it, between 50 and 54. Yet William Grant – mathematician, accountant, diplomat – seemed utterly perplexed, peering up at numberplates, crossing and criss-crossing the road between the odds and the evens, taking a few steps back, then coming forward again.

Her mother watched him, the first sight of her old lover in nearly forty years, and said: —You know his problem? Needs glasses.

A silence between them as they hovered over William.

Then Morag couldn't stop herself from asking: —Why didn't you go with him?

Her mother looked at her for a moment, surprised at

her directness, then turned and stared out the window at William. Tilted her head like a curious dog.

—You never answered Dad's question.

She still glared down into the street, as if the absent-minded, short-sighted William below had posed the question. Then she spoke quietly, misting up the window pane.

—How can you go anywhere with someone who hardly exists?

Screwing up her eyes, as if William might indeed be fading away. So insubstantial you had to peer hard just to make him out. His grey suit in the dun-grey street below.

—I used to want to take him and bang his head against the walls.

And automatically put her hand to the back of her head, fingers looking for the scar left by the boy who had struck her against the hard reality of the city. Downstairs, William had at last worked out which flat was Morag's, was crossing back over the street, heading for the close door.

—That's why I ran after him.

Morag was shocked, and Grace drew her head away slightly, as though her daughter might lash out at her.

—*You* ran after *him*?

The bell rang. Neither of the two women paid it any mind.

—I knew the minute I cast eyes on him you could do anything with a man like William, and it'd be like it'd never even happened. George, on the other hand, existed too much.

The bell rang again. This time, both woman glanced towards the living-room door, but neither of them made a move towards it.

—William was a non-person. It felt like freedom, being with him. Like taking off something tight.

Morag looked down into the street. William had his ear up close to the intercom speaker and was studying his watch.

—How did Dad find out?

—I told him. It was the only way of pulling myself back. It worked. I've never slipped away since.

The bell rang a third time. Morag and her mother glanced at one another, decided, without speaking, that Morag was the one who should go and speak to him. Out in the hall, she picked up the intercom phone at the main door and asked him to wait for a few minutes. She'd be down as soon as she could.

Inside the living room again, her mother had moved to a chair in front of the mantelpiece. Morag sat beside her. They made no further mention of William nor discussed whether or not Grace should go down to meet him. Instead they made conversation about Morag's plans to go away.

—You're sure you'll go, then?

—Can't think of a reason why not. Can you?

Grace brushed the crumbs from her lap, rubbed at a little spill of tea on her saucer with her pinkie, moved in that jerky way she always did.

—If you don't like it, there's nothing to stop you coming back.

—And if I do like it, and stay? Would you miss me?

Grace nodded, and so did Morag.

—We'll write.

—I'd still come home whenever I could.

Then Morag gathered herself up, perched on the edge of her chair and said she'd better go down and see William. Grace said she'd clear up and let herself out.

Downstairs, on the street, William offered Morag his arm and she took it, glanced back up at her top-storey window. True enough, there was Mum looking out, half hiding behind the curtain.

William consented to Morag's plan in nearly every detail. By Thursday he'd made all the essential calls and it didn't look as if there was going to be a problem. He'd phoned Libertina at home and told her the daughter of an old friend of his was coming out, would like to work for a while as a nurse there. Libertina had insisted on her staying with her and, yes she was sure there'd be a way of finding a job for the woman. Never too many nurses in a country like this. William was to tell her that John, Libertina's husband, would drive out to Walvis Bay when her boat got in and take her back to Windhoek. Libertina was very much looking forward to meeting her. She even wondered if when Morag first got there she might consider helping to look after Libertina's kids. Morag told William to tell Libertina she'd be honoured.

Morag left the sale of the house with her lawyer, purchased her plane ticket to Liverpool and organised her travel from there to the port. She called the Namibian Embassy in London and spoke to the man William had put her on to. By Friday, it looked as if there was very little to do but pack. She phoned Michael and told him, just in case he was ever looking for her. He sounded harassed and busy and said, 'Yeah OK thanks. Good for you. How are you anyway?' Morag felt a little sorry for him, and worried he might be working himself into an early grave. —Fuckwit, she said and hung up.

Africa. Despite her tenuous, but lifelong, connection with the continent, it had never dawned on Morag ever actually to go there. If anyone, only a few weeks ago, had told her she'd end up in Africa one day, she'd've laughed out loud. All Africa was to her was a name. A name that managed to imply brightness and darkness simultaneously, hope and the lack of it. Massive place. Big woman though Morag was, she'd still only be a tiny, blonde little dot on that landmass. The sheer space and her newness to it made Africa the ideal place for a woman in her situation.

She'd work. Of course she would. Work hard, like she always did. But she'd also do all those things that one does in a place like Africa. She'd see the wildlife. Travel. Safaris, that kind of thing. There'd be so much to do and see, and she was already halfway through her life, that she could easily fill up what was left with Africa. All she'd need'd be a few colleagues – people to tell what she had done and seen. A few patients to look after, money to pay for a roof and food, weekend trips. Heat and light.

—After all, I could have been an African child, she said to William, and he said that was never really on the cards, Morag.

Morag spent the next few days in a whirlwind of phoning, writing, organising. Her lawyer and her mother between them would take care of most things including the sale of the flat, storage of her things and sending on stuff that she needed. She went to the doctor's and got the last of her vaccinations. She visited her mother every day, making up in advance for the time they soon wouldn't have together. The boat that William had organised for her left next week. She ought to feel panicked, start worrying about all the things she hadn't done, but she didn't. William kept trying to convince her to stay. Told her that this country had so much going for it. Africa's deceptive, he said. It promises and threatens all the time. Plays tricks on the eye and the mind. Where there seems to be peace, there's not and what seems innocent can be deadly. Morag said it sounded brill.

—My father, William said, as he made his farewell to Morag before setting off in search of the island that his grandfather and father and Uncle Robert had hailed from, – always thanked God for this soft, temperate climate. Keeps everything in balance, in check. Everything in moderation.

Morag asked William if he'd like her to set up a meeting – a proper one this time, no tricks – with her mother.

—Did Grace ask for such a meeting? he asked.

—No.

—In that case, no.

—I'll see you there, then, I suppose. In Namibia, she said, and he didn't respond, but nodded to her, and in that nod there was a kind of finality. He turned away, but then stopped and spoke. Not to her so much, she felt, but to the streets around about her. To the city itself.

—It's taken me all my life to figure out why he loved this place so fiercely. My dad. I thought he was seeing things that weren't there. The March of Progress, Greatest Education System in the World. Fair-minded People. I've spent sixty years trying to work it out and it's only recently I've realised that it doesn't matter a damn if he was right or wrong. Maybe sheer faith in these things makes them possible. Perhaps all that holds any country together are the stories it tells itself. I'd thought there were no dreams here. But it was just that I had to go away to dream them.

Then he turned and faced Morag.

—Tell your mother I got beyond the lowest common denominator.

He turned away without another wave or word. Poor man, she thought: spending time wandering around a foreign city, searching for a woman he'd never find. He hadn't been able to make the first move forty years ago and couldn't make the last move now.

On the day before Morag left for Africa, she and her mother went out walking and Morag led her up Kelso Street and into Bunnahabhain Road, right past number 29. Grace didn't stop her, or complain, but followed dutifully. At the gate of the old semidetached house, both women waved and smiled at a toddler who played on a swing in the newly landscaped garden. Grace looked in through the living-room window, as if searching for something that would connect this house with the one she used to visit on Saturday mornings. Then she glanced up at the upstairs bedroom, and winced.

—George was right. What a dire figure I must have cut.

Age and time hadn't saved her from the odious moistenings and humiliating loosenings of her body that still accompanied that revolting image of herself. Those ancient Saturday mornings had become a recurring nightmare for her.

—The funny thing is, she said, and made an effort to return the little girl on the swing's wave and smile, —William's not there in my memory.

She tried to laugh.

—Nearly everyone else is, though. I still wake up sometimes, in the middle of the night, and think I'm there again. Displaying myself as if there was something worth displaying. And there's a whole gallery of folk watching me. Isobel, George. My own mother.

—And two of you, Morag. The four-year-old version, and the way you are now. Everyone's standing gawping at me. The whole damned city seeing me for what I really am.

—I've never been ashamed of you, Morag said, and

although both of them knew it was a lie, it was important that she said it then.

Morag took her mother by the arm and led her away from number 29. She felt her relax as they turned the crook of the road into Patrick Brae, and on to the top of Policy Street hill, where her mother had been attacked and where Paris McFarlane had thought she'd been as she lay dying. They stood there, mother and daughter on their last day together, looking down over the river that moved invisibly along below.

Morag told her mother for the first time how the hilltop breeze, when it brushes her face, always makes her think of Paris gliding past. She'd never mentioned her vision before. Now she explained how it was just a trick of the light. Or, rather the lack of light. The clouds at this time of year blindfold the sky, and the slush and the mist leach the daylight out of the city. Everything loses its shape, and you think you see things. Things like a desperate boy's panic, a dying girl's dream. A mother's regret.

From this vantage point Morag could see the whole of that little world, from the backs of the small tenements that she lived in halfway down the hill, and over Dudhope and the decaying old villas to the Golden Triangle. The further up the hill you got, the more the houses cost. Isobel Grant paid with her sanity. William with a lifetime of exile. Her own mother held on to her property thanks to a lifetime of thrift and deceit and vengeance. Such a quiet, modest little grouping of streets, yet their shadow stretched and fell for thousands of miles, as far as Africa, India, America.

—D'you know the last thing I ever said to him?

Both women were thinking of George. How many thousands of hours had they spent together with George Lapraik on their minds and never uttering his name?

—I went into his room late at night. The night the doctor'd been, remember? I knelt down beside his bed. I leant over him, swept my hair away from his face. What age would I be – fourteen? I stroked his cheek and said: 'Die, Daddy. Please die.'

Grace looked at her, astonished.

—My God.

Morag averted her eyes, ashamed. But when she looked up, her mother was smiling. Amazed and still a little shocked, beginning to giggle. Morag laughed too. Not at George. Not at what had happened, but thanks to the lightness she felt after confessing to something that had laid heavily on her for years.

Then she remembered something else. While Dad was still alive, and Morag was very small. Being on this spot, or hereabouts, with her mother. It must've been in William's time. Mum was in a good mood that day and picked her up and flew her around in a circle, both of them shouting Wheee. Remembering this, Morag drew her mother close to her in a hug, and shuffled her around, and they laughed.

Moving around like that, peering over Grace's shoulder, Morag got fleeting glimpses of the hill, the sky, Paris's red plum tree, the top of Bunnahabhain Road, the back of Arran House, home for children at risk. The whole scene gave her a sense of elation.

That vision of hers – three people rising up towards the dank clouds – no longer frightened her. Doesn't matter whether she really saw it or not, there was nothing to be scared of.

Three people getting themselves tangled up in low-hanging clouds. Morag tried to imagine what it must be like up there. To float freely, see her city from far above, breathe air uncontaminated with vicious words.

Eventually, Morag and Grace had to let go of one another and the vision faded in the mist. Mother and daughter separated slowly, turning to wave every few seconds, Grace heading west, via Bunnahabhain Road. Morag, south, down the hill.

Halfway down, the rain came on and the sky darkened. Morag saw people scurrying along the main street below, putting on hats and pulling on scarves and hoisting umbrellas, all of them glancing up at the threatening March sky, waiting for the heavens to open.